FALLEN

a short story collection

I0626377

Also by J.B. Hogan

The Rubicon: Poetry and Short Fiction
Losing Cotton
Living Behind Time
Angels In The Ozarks
The Apostate

FALLEN

a short story collection

J.B. HOGAN

LIFFEY PRESS

AN IMPRINT OF
OGHMA CREATIVE MEDIA

ISBN: 978-1-63373-127-1

Interior Design and Editing by Casey W. Cowan

Liffey Press
Oghma Creative Media
Fayetteville, AR 72703
www.oghmacreative.com

"California or Bust" appeared in *Underground Voices*.

"Police Action: October 17, 1951," "Just Waiting on You, Gordon" (as "Last Flight"), and "Drinking the Revolution" appeared in the *Copperfield Review*.

"They Give Bank Robbing a Bad Name," "Stormy Weather," "Train Boarding," and "Fallen" appeared in *Cynic Online Magazine*.

"Waiting for Jesus" and "Ozark Beats" appeared in *Dead Mule*.

"Papi" appeared in *The Square Table*.

"Time Pieces: Something Lost—A Night of Stars" appeared in *Megaera*.

"Field Work" appeared in the *Fayetteville Free Weekly*.

"At a Station on the Metro" originally appeared in the *Istanbul Literary Review*.

"For Bread and Milk" appeared in *The Square Table* and in *ken*again*.

"Still Life: Girl on Snowy Night" appeared in *The Square Table* and with "Morena," "Up from Matagalpa" and "A Near Love Story" in the chapbook *Near Love Stories* published online by Cervena Barva Press.

contents

I want to thank the following for giving me permission to fictionalize their remarkable stories:

My brother Bill Hogan for the wild one about the men trying to get to California.

My cousin Larry Fultz for sharing the poignant juxtaposition of combat and friendship in Viet Nam.

My friend Roger Serrette for the sometimes humorous perils of the Tokyo train system.

I think that's all.

J. B.

Dedicated to my cousin:

Roy "Teenie" Allen

KIA, Korea, October 17, 1951

"The snares of the world were its ways of sin. He would fall. He had not yet fallen but he would fall silently, in an instant. Not to fall was too hard, too hard: and he felt the silent lapse of his soul, as it would be at some instant to come, falling, falling but not yet fallen, still unfallen but about to fall."

James Joyce
A Portrait of the Artist as a Young Man

California or Bust

If Mick Sullivan hadn't thrown all those rocks at all those know-it-all psychologists and got himself thrown out of the state home and if the stray dogs hadn't moved into his run down one-room house by the city dump and drove him out to the chicken shed where the mangy mutts had been living, he and Tommy Ryan wouldn't have had to come up with a plan to go to California.

"They just tooken over the house," Mick told Tommy by way of explaining the dogs' new digs. "Ate up all my food and just started layin' all over. I had to come out here to this little old chicken house to find any peace of mind."

"I reckon it could happen to anybody," Tommy rubbed the stubble on his dirty chin.

"Hell, yes," Mick confirmed. "Happened to me."

"What are you gonna do?" Tommy wondered.

"I ain't come up with a plan yet. Got any ideers?"

Tommy leaned back in his chair and one leg gave way, dumping him onto the filthy, nearly petrified remains of chicken feed, chicken excrement, and chicken feathers on the floor of the shed.

"Damn," he said, picking himself up. He tried to wipe his hands off but his own clothes were so threadbare and dirty that it was a waste of effort.

"You gotta watch them there chairs," Mick belatedly warned his second or third cousin or something removed cousin or step-cousin or whatever it was that Tommy was to him, relative-wise.

"I can see that," Tommy carefully propped the now three-legged chair up against a wall where he could semi-safely sit in it again.

Mick started to ask Tommy again if he had any "ideers" about what to do about the dogs and all but he was interrupted by the arrival of a couple of small dogs—no doubt new strays that didn't know or had forgotten that the doghouse was Mick's old house and that the cramped chicken house was the new human house where the put-upon scion of railroad Irish now lived. Feeling both physically and psychologically penned in by the newest canine interlopers, Mick and Tommy chased the yelping mutts away.

"Damned fleabags," Tommy cursed after the animals. "You oughta do somethin' about that."

"What can I do?" Mick wailed. "They just come in my house and kept comin' until they made me leave."

"Fleabags," Tommy repeated, "nothin' but fleabags."

"You're tellin' me," Mick sadly nodded his head.

"You oughta do somethin' about it," Tommy said again.

"If the damned mutts is goin' to take over my house and this chicken shed, too," Mick speculated, "I'll be out on my ass. Nowhere to stay. Except under a bridge or somethin'."

"I don't like doin' that," Tommy commented, clearly from personal experience.

"It ain't no fun," Mick agreed.

The two men sat still for a few moments, cogitating on the problem and nodding their heads back and forth like they were considering good, reasonable ways for Mick to get out from under his dog problem. There had to be something they could do. Finally, Tommy stood up with a flourish.

"I got a idea," he said.

"You do?" Mick asked doubtfully.

"Yes, sir," Tommy said, "I got me one."

"Well," Mick said, "what is it? You gonna just set there thinkin' and not tellin' me?"

"Do somethin' crazy to get yourself put back into that crazy house place," Tommy announced proudly.

"That's your ideer?" Mick said, astonished. "You know I cain't go back in there. They done tossed me out forever. Throwin' them rocks got me banned, they said. For life, too."

"Why did you do that, anyways?" Tommy asked.

"It ain't no never mind to you," Mick replied. "I just did and they didn't like it and they tossed me out. Simple as that. That's all they wuz."

"Seems kind of nutty to have throwed rocks at your doctors and all," Tommy allowed.

"What do you care why I done it?" Mick asked. "'Sides, I thought we was talkin' about getting out of this dumb shed."

"Just wonderin'."

"Get another ideer. Try somethin' else."

Tommy pondered the problem again. He scratched his stubbly chin. He pulled on one of his ears. He tried to knock some sort of dried, hard feces – chicken or dog, he couldn't tell – off one of his thin-soled formerly working boots.

"C'mon, c'mon," Mick yelled at him.

"Alright," Tommy said, "I thought of somethin' else."

"Tell me."

"You gotta move, find somewheres else to live. That's it. Just get the heck out and leave this all to the dogs."

"Move?" Mick wondered, scratching his own stubbly chin. "I never thought of that. Where would I go?"

"California," Tommy pronounced the state name like it was a secret word in some magical incantation.

"California," Mick echoed breathlessly. "California."

The men looked at each other as if they had just spoken the words that would grant them leave to enter the gates of heaven. But Mick had a quick sobering thought.

"How we gonna get there?" he asked.

"Well, hell," Tommy said, as if it were the most obvious thing in the world to anybody in the world, "we'll drive. We'll drive to California."

"Yeah," Mick said, "yeah. But...how?"

"In cars," Tommy explained, "or your truck."

"My truck?"

"Sure, you gotta good truck, don't you?"

"It runs good. Burns some oil. But it runs."

"There you go then."

"It ain't got no brakes," Mick lamented.

If his truck just had brakes they could head right off for California. Why did the master cylinder have to go out on that damned truck last year anyway? That didn't seem fair, or right.

"Life ain't fair," he complained.

"I got me another ideer," Tommy's eyes widened from the onslaught of another great thought. "You know my old Dodge?"

"Yeah?"

"Well, it's got real good brakes. The engine block's got a crack in it, but the brakes is real good. Don't squeal or nothing."

"Yeah?"

"Well."

Mick thought this new proposal over. It seemed like a real good plan. Except for one thing.

"There's one thing I don't get. What good is it we have two automobiles with one good thing about each one but the two ain't....oh...oh. We hook the darn things together!"

"Now you're talkin'," Tommy cheered. "We hook 'em together."

"What with?" Mick asked, mostly of himself.

"I didn't get that far," Tommy admitted.

Mick went to the door of the shed and looked out at the nearby junk yard. He shook his head and whistled.

"Follow me," he told Tommy. "I done figured out how we can do it."

• • •

"What in the hell are you two dumbheads doin'," George Sullivan laughed when he saw the contraption his weak-minded step-brother Mick and their barely stronger-minded step-cousin Tommy had put together out of parts and supplies from the city junkyard. "What is that supposed to be?"

"I ain't talkin' to you, George," Mick bowed his head as if George would smack him a good one across the side of the face like he'd made a lifetime habit of doing. "You leave me alone."

"I ought to kick both of your asses from here to Neosho," George laughed. He made feinted with his right hand that caused Mick to jump back from his bigger, tougher, and all-around meaner step-brother. "You won't get five miles from town with that idiotic thing."

"Why won't we, George?" Tommy asked seriously. "They's hooked together real good. And we got plenty of gas and oil from old cars in the junkyard. Mick found all that and the chain we used here."

"If you don't run up against each other and blow yourselves to hell, the law'll pitch both of your idiot butts in jail, day one," George laughed.

"They ain't nothin' illegal we doin'," Tommy countered.

"We're goin' to California," Mick added.

"You're goin' straight to hell, as far I'm concerned," George shook his head.

"Naw, we're goin' to California, George," Tommy reassured his rough step-cousin.

"We're leavin' this place today," Mick said firmly.

"Don't forget to take your damned dogs," George growled.

"Ain't takin' them," Mick said, embarrassed.

"Well piss on both of you," George said with disgust. "I hope you both do go to hell and take that thing with you. You dumbasses."

"He don't understand," Tommy told Mick as George stomped away.

"He's just plain mean," Mick said. "Been that way his whole life. Good riddance to him."

"Let's get started," Tommy suggested, "and get out of this here place."

"I'm for that," Mick said, "let's go."

• • •

Mick and Tommy got out of Ash Hill and onto Highway 71 North about three-thirty in the afternoon. Usually managing about fifteen miles an hour and keeping their chain-linked vehicular contraption to the far right of the road to let faster cars zoom past them, they made it to the outskirts of Rich Hill, just about nineteen miles north of Ash Hill, a little before five p.m.

"What are them people lookin' at, Mick?" Tommy called out the window of the Dodge, as the residents of Rich Hill, noting the peculiar-looking dual vehicle passing by, began to congregate alongside the highway to stare, gawk, and wave.

Mick leaned his head out the window of the pickup and cupped a hand over his ear to let Tommy know he couldn't hear him. Tommy pointed to the gathering crowd beyond the road. Mick craned his neck for a better view. Some of the people seemed to be laughing, others were cheering, a couple of little boys had a rope and were pulling each other around in apparent imitation of the Sullivan-Ryan combination engine, brake-mobile.

"Let's stop here for the night," Mick suggested, turning the pickup onto the road leading into town.

Tommy carefully applied the brakes to keep them from roaring into town too fast, which as far as he was concerned was anything over about ten miles an hour. Sometimes Mick had pushed the truck up to as much as twenty miles an hour, which seemed just downright reckless to Tommy.

In Rich Hill, the two men were treated like celebrities. When it was discovered they only had an onion and bologna sandwich apiece for eating and some brackish looking water in a plastic bottle, a couple of local women brought them a decent meal of meatloaf and vegetables and some good Samaritan offered them thirst-quenching bottles of beer.

Everyone wanted to know where they were going and how they'd thought up their tandem vehicles. It all went well until about bedtime when a couple of young roughs suggested in no uncertain terms that Mick and Tommy were stark-raving idiots and a hazard to public driving. Mick started to collect some rocks to throw at the boys but Tommy and one of the nice ladies restrained him. Calm was restored and the travelers spent the rest of the night in their vehicles in peace.

Next day they made it all the way to Harrisonville, south of Kansas City – despite frequent stops to tighten the chain, not to mention the oil that had to be added to the pickup engine or the flat tire they had to fix—but the second day they barely got to Grandview, still south of the big city.

The people of Grandview gave them a reception almost like the folks in Rich Hill had but with one difference: here the local toughs actually got physical with Mick and Tommy and they had to drive two or three miles outside of town to get a night's sleep. Tommy allowed that at their current pace, it might take a spell to get to California.

"We ain't got nothin' but time," Mick reassured him, as they sat on the tailgate of the pickup and looked up at the moon and stars shining down on west-central Missouri.

"Wouldn't be bad to get there 'fore next year," Tommy said petulantly.

"It were your ideer," Mick reminded his step-cousin. "You was the one what wanted to go to California."

"Didn't know it would take so long," Tommy replied.

"We get there a whole lot sooner if you'd let me drive faster," Mick said.

He couldn't understand Tommy's fear of not being able to brake the pickup. Shoot, that chain would stop him at fifty miles an hour, Mick was sure of that.

"It ain't the speed so much no more," Tommy said, "as all the stoppin'. And I ain't too keen on how people is behavin' at us neither."

"They been right friendly, mostly."

"Yeah, that's why we is out here in the middle of nowhere with no hot food and nobody but our ownselves to talk to."

"We can turn back if you want," Mick said, "but ...."

"Naw, I wadn't sayin' that," Tommy backed up a bit. "I was just thinkin' how nice it would be if we could get on out to California. See them orange trees and stuff. The ocean and all."

"We'll make 'er," Mick said optimistically. "This two-machine deal is goin' to work just fine. We'll be out there 'fore you know it."

"Sure we will," Tommy said, buoyed by the image of a land filled with food and easy labor for high wages just days beyond his reach. The land of milk and honey, he thought, manna from heaven like it says in the Bible.

● ● ●

The following day Mick and Tommy actually made it through Kansas City. Despite Tommy's insistence that they should turn west at Kansas City in order to go straight to California, Mick was equally insistent that Highway 71 was the only road that could possibly get them through Kansas City safe and sound. It was late in the day when the motorcycle patrolman signaled for the two travelers to pull their vehicles over to the side of the road just a couple of miles south of Platte City.

The officer wore tall, storm-trooper black leather boots that came almost to his knees. His uniform was solid black or deep, deep blue. He wore a blue helmet with a gold badge painted on the front. He removed his thick black gloves as he walked towards Mick and Tommy's joined vehicles, his solid jaw jutting out like a challenge to all the Perps in the world who might mistake him for a soft touch.

At his side, a semi-automatic, 9-millimeter Glock was carefully strapped into its holster. The weapon stood out from the policeman's utility belt, which had several hard leather pockets, snapped firmly shut and filled, no doubt, with ammo clips and other items designed to keep the errant citizenry in line. A mace can was held in place on his left hip by a Velcro strap. The officer was well prepared for any roadside emergency.

As he walked up and down the length of the two vehicles, the officer shook his head a couple of times, scratched his chin, and sighed deeply. Mick and Tommy tried to surreptitiously signal one another but their efforts were thwarted by the proximity of the somewhat perplexed but alert officer. After making two or three trips from one end of the linked vehicles to the other, the patrolman finally stopped just beyond Mick's door where both men could easily see and hear him.

"Do you gentlemen know why I stopped you?" he asked calmly.

"Uh..." Mick began.

"We was just goin'," Tommy interrupted, "to California."

"You intended to tow this vehicle all that way?" the officer asked incredulously.

"Yes, sir," Mick said.

"All the way," Tommy said with conviction, "to California."

"Uh, yeah, I got that part," the officer said.

"It's not really towin'," Mick added, "so much as it is pullin'."

"I'm sorry?" the policeman replied, raising an eyebrow.

"See I got a good motor in this here pickup," Mick explained, "and Tommy's got good breaks on his car back there. Together it's a real sweet truck-car."

The officer scratched his forehead and sighed again.

"You wouldn't happen to have driver's licenses, registration, proof of insurance – that sort of thing would you?" he asked.

"Somewhere's in here," Mick answered, beginning to dig around the glove compartment of the pickup.

"I didn't think I needed none," Tommy called up, as Mick held out some paperwork for the policeman.

"Thank you, sir," the officer said. "If you gentlemen will remain in your vehicles with your engines, er, engine off, I'll be right back."

As the patrolman walked back to his motorcycle, Mick and Tommy resumed their waving back and forth. Neither could understand what the other's arm-flailing signals meant.

"What do you reckon he's checkin' on," Tommy finally just said, in the loudest low voice he could manage and still be heard.

"Hush, now," Mick said, "I can hear him on his radio."

"Well, what's he sayin'?"

"Sounds like they done heard of us. Somebody or other called in about us to 'em."

"Yeah?"

"Yeah, and ... wait, the motorcycle cop is gettin' red-faced."

"How come?"

"Somethin' about vehicle traveling violations and ... oh, no, tickets, I heard tickets."

"We cain't pay no tickets," Tommy said, "we ain't hardly got enough to go to California as it is."

"Hush up," Mick waved for Tommy to be quiet, "listen."

"...to deal with them," the men heard the patrolman say into his hand-held radio, "...standard procedure .... what am I supposed to ... well, hell ... yes, sir, yes, sir ... I don't see how .... yes, sir, if that's what you want."

"Uh, oh," Mick fretted, "here he comes back."

"It seems, gentlemen," the patrolman said when he had made his way back to the pair of linked vehicles and drivers, "that we have something of a precedent here."

"A what?" Tommy asked, with a blank expression. The police officer's face flushed and he rattled Mick's papers.

"I don't believe," the patrolman said through clenched teeth and ignoring Tommy's question, "that there is a single traffic law that you two have not violated here today in my jurisdiction."

"I know what that means," Tommy said with a crooked smile.

"Yes, well," the officer went on, his grip on Mick's papers tightening, "it seems that my superiors feel the best thing to do here is to allow you gentlemen to continue on with your, uh, journey."

"That mean we can go?" Mick wondered. The patrolman leaned back, adjusted his shoulders as if they had a kink in them and then glared down at Mick.

"Don't think for one second that that's what I would like to see happen here," he said, the grinding of his molars almost palpable.

"You not gonna write us no ticket?" Tommy asked. "We can just go?"

"Yes," the policeman said firmly, "and if it were me, I'd be going right now."

Mick started the pickup. Tommy tested the brakes on the Dodge. They both looked at the officer. The veins on his neck bulged.

"What are you waiting on?" he asked the travelers.

"Can I ... I have my papers back?" Mick said timidly. For a moment it looked like the policeman might draw his revolver and end the trip on the spot. "Please," Mick added, "Mr. Sir."

The officer shoved the papers at Mick. Tommy beeped his horn for Mick to take off. The patrolman stepped back away from the dual-vehicle contraption. He took a deep, long breath.

"Get this damned thing out of my county," the officer barked at Mick and Tommy, "on the double, you understand me? I don't care where you go. I don't care how you get there. Just get yourselves and this thing out of my jurisdiction – and don't come back, ever."

"No, sir," Mick said, "we'll be sure not to do that."

"See that you don't."

Mick shoved the pickup in gear and waved back to Tommy to release the brake. With a blast of black and blue smoke, the pickup lurched forward pulling the chain taught between it and the Dodge. The two vehicles began to slowly lumber up the highway. The exasperated patrolman stepped back and watched the vehicles move away with a final shake of his head.

"Hot damn," Mick cheered, leaning out the window as the officer walked back to his motorcycle, "California or Bust!"

"Let's go," Tommy yelped from the Dodge.

He was so glad to be clear of the law that the fact they were going north and not west no longer seemed to matter much to him. He let out a big hoot and a holler of joy and leaned his head out the window to yell up to Mick.

"California here we come!" he cried. "California or Bust!"

"Hot damn," Mick cried out happily, "yee ha!"

Behind them, the patrolman started his motorcycle, hammered it in gear, and then shot out onto the highway heading south as fast as he could go. In seconds he was far down the road, nearly out of sight, his motorcycle rumbling loudly into the still Missouri air. He never once looked back.

Happily back on course for California, Mick and Tommy kept up a steady, if slow, pace. With any luck they'd make it to St. Joe in the next day or two and from there they'd figure out which direction it was to get out west. They weren't too worried. They had enough gas and food to last for a while. As far as they were concerned, it was just a matter of avoiding local bullies and the police and it would be clear sailing to the coast. California or Bust was the plan – and, by doggies, they were sticking to it.

They Give Bank Robbing a Bad Name

"Henry," Aunt Margaret called from the kitchen.

I sat on the big heavy couch in her living room, trying to stay cool and reading the motion picture ads in the newspaper.

"Yes, ma'am?"

"Would you please go to Brown's Grocery for me before your folks and your Uncle Charley get back from Rogers?"

I set the newspaper on an end table and stood up. "What do you want me to get, Aunt Margaret?"

It was pretty hot in the little house and the idea of going to the store, where they would have cold Coca-Colas on ice, sounded okay to me. Maybe there would be a breeze outside, too.

"I need a brick of cheese and some ham. Maybe two pounds." Aunt Margaret came into the living room. "And a can of those nice peaches in syrup."

"Boy that sounds good." I imagined the wonderful food Aunt Margaret planned for evening.

My folks and dad's brother Charley would be back pretty soon and we'd have supper. Later I hoped to go see an Edward G. Robinson movie. It was called *Little Caesar* and was bound to be real exciting. It was going to be a great weekend in town.

"Here's a dollar." Aunt Margaret handed me four quarters.

"I'll bring back the change, if there is any."

"You should get a little back, and go ahead and get yourself a Coca-Cola if you want."

"Thanks, Aunt Margaret," I smiled.

She was the best aunt. Always nice to me. Cooked real good, too. And always let me get treats whenever I did something for her. Her and Charley were about as good an aunt and uncle as a fellow could have. I really liked coming into town to visit them. Sometimes I spent a whole week. I would go up to the square, and out to the ballpark, and just do whatever I wanted. It was great getting away from all the chores out home in the country.

"Hurry on, now. They'll be here soon enough."

"Yes, ma'am." I put the quarters in the pocket of my favorite brown trousers I always wore to town.

Outside it was even hotter than I expected. There were a lot of shade trees on Washington Avenue—oaks, elms, and maples—but not much wind, and anywhere there wasn't a tree the sun was pretty hot. It had been a dry summer, especially for around here, and only a couple of clouds in the sky didn't help much with any cooling down. I walked down to the corner of Lafayette Street hopping from shade to shade. The old trees in that part of town were so big it didn't take much hopping to just about stay out of the direct sunlight.

At Lafayette I switched over onto the south side of the road and walked west, into the sun, towards Highway 71, which was also College Street. There wasn't hardly any shade there and the sun beat down something awful. I walked briskly to the corner and, lucky enough, there weren't any cars on the highway so I just crossed there and kept going west. The road had a kind of rise in it there where it ran below the part of town they called Mt. Nord. I walked slow then, looking for shade but not finding much until I got to the next corner. Straight ahead was Brown's Grocery.

Brown's was in the shade, it being close to five-thirty and all, and because of these two really tall old oak trees just west of the store. The building's thick wooden door was propped open, and I pulled back the screen door and went right in. It was cool in there. Besides the shade from the trees, the Brown's had a big fan by a window spreading the air around. That fan was a newfangled kind and it swung back and forth on its own. I watched that for a while before I remembered why I had come in the first place.

I easy enough picked up the can of peaches Aunt Margaret wanted off a shelf, but thought I'd wait a minute on the ham and cheese 'cause it might get too hot on the walk back home. I was thinking about having me a nice cold Coca-Cola right there in the store before I got the other stuff. Tossing the peach can around in my hands for fun, I walked over to the ice chest and looked inside. There was a whole bunch of soft drinks in there: oranges and strawberries and about a dozen cold Coca-Colas—co-colas Aunt Margaret sometimes called them.

I dug around in the cold water and ice, letting my hands get good and cold, too, before I pulled one of them Coca-Colas out that was pretty near froze. I knew it was going to taste great. I opened it with the opener that was on the left side of the ice chest and took a big long swallow. It was so cold, it made me wince and my head and eyes hurt. Ewell Trammell, who worked for Brown's as a delivery boy and such, laughed when he saw my face all crinkled up.

"Better take her easy there, buddy," he kidded me, looking over at Mrs. Brown, who shook her head like grownups do when they see kids do dumb stuff.

"I'm okay." I pretended like my head wasn't still hurting.

I took another big drink, but got lucky and didn't get any more cold headache from it. Ewell laughed again and went into the back of the store. He came back out with a broom and dustpan.

"I'm goin' to sweep up a bit, Mrs. Brown," he told the owner.

I didn't see Mr. Brown anywhere, so I figured he was in back, too, or maybe up on the square doing business of some kind. I was just guessing.

I had drunk about half of my Coca-Cola when the man came into the store. It was close to exactly five-thirty because I had just seen the clock at one side of the counter by the cash register and was admiring the neat numbers on the big time piece. The numbers looked like they were in some kind of old-time writing or something. I reckoned they were Roman numerals, but I wasn't too sure. Next to the clock was a calendar that had a picture of a new Ford car on it. It was June 23, 1932.

I'll never forget that.

The guy who came in didn't look like he was from around here, even though I was a visitor in town myself. Just something about him that was different. I also noticed out a side window that there was a four-door Ford Sedan out front, and it had another man in it. He kept jerking his head around around as if he was looking for somebody, but never got out of the car.

The man that came in was pretty rough looking, too. Unshaven, wearing a brown shirt and blue trousers. I figured him for about twenty-five, thirty years old—but I can't always tell how old grownups are. I had a funny feeling about this guy, so I sidled off to about midway back in the store and acted like I was reading labels on the canned food.

"Can I help you, sir?" Mrs. Brown asked, real friendly and polite like.

The man didn't say anything at first, he just kind of looked around like he was searching for something particular in the store maybe. He seemed to be acting a little odd, a little funny, but I didn't make too much of it at first.

"May I help you, sir?" Mrs. Brown asked again.

He looked up this time and acted like he was going to speak. Ewell stopped his sweeping and watched the guy. I kind of slid back against the shelves closer to the back of the store.

"Yes, you can," the fellow finally said to Mrs. Brown kinda of peculiar-like. A little rough, bossy sort of, like making fun of someone. "You can help me real good."

"How's that, sir?" Mrs. Brown raised an eyebrow. Then she said, "Oh, my," real sudden like.

I looked up, and so did Ewell. We both froze where we were. The fellow had pulled out a pistol. A big pistol. A heavy, black pistol. I'd seen them before like that. I knew it was one of those .45s like the army carries. Looking at that pistol made me wish I'd never come to town at all, much less to Brown's grocery.

"This is a stickup. I want all the money in your till."

"Sir," Mrs. Brown, said, "please. We barely make ends meet as it is. Take some food if you need but don't rob us."

The man looked around the store really fast. He looked nervous and that made all of us nervous, too.

"We don't take in much in a day," Mrs. Brown said. "Do we, Ewell?"

"Uh...n..., no ma'am," Ewell blurted out. I could tell he was scared to death.

"Stop blabbin'," the man said, all excitable-like, "and give me your money."

"But, sir..." Mrs. Brown began.

"Shut up, old woman," the man said, waving his .45 around in the air. "Get out of the way."

He stomped up to the front of the store and shoved Mrs. Brown. She made a little crying sound but got out of the way. The man pulled open the drawer of the register—it was one of those older ones that didn't ring up sales—and grabbed all the money out, holding the bills in one hand and putting all the coins in his pants pocket. He counted it quick, pointing that .45 all over the place while he did.

"There ain't maybe thirty dollars in here," he said angry-like to Mrs. Brown. "You got anymore anywhere else? You got a safe somewhere?"

"That's all we have, sir. Please don't take it. We're just a poor little store."

"Where's the safe?" The man pointed the .45 at Ewell.

"They ain't one, sir," Ewell managed to get out. I could see his knees wobbling from across the room. "You got everything."

"What you got on you, boy?" The man came out from behind the counter and headed straight for Ewell. I thought Ewell was going to pass out. While the guy was hollering at Ewell, I slipped my quarters behind some cans of peas on a shelf near where I was standing.

"I don't have any money, sir," Ewell pleaded. "Honest."

"What's in your pockets?" The man frisked Ewell on the outside of his clothes.

"I just got some change." Ewell held out his hand.

"Gimme that." The man grabbed the coins out of Ewell's hands. I was really glad I had hid mine.

"Thirty-five damned cents. What a cheap outfit."

"I ain't got no more," Ewell said meekly.

"What about you, boy?" The man turned his mean look on me.

"I ain't got nothin' at all, mister," I lied to beat the band.

"Am I gonna have to come over and frisk you, too, sonny?" the man threatened.

"No, sir." I turned my pants pockets inside out.

The man suddenly turned on Ewell like he had a big idea or something. Ewell jumped back like he was going to get shot.

"There a delivery truck or some kind of automobile around here?"

He peered out the store windows. The other fellow was still out there in that car. I could see he was still looking around as if watching for someone or something. To one side of the car, I could see an old truck with a small flatbed. I figured that was the Brown's delivery truck, if they had one.

"Yes...sir," Ewell finally answered. "That old truck is it."

"Does it need a key?"

"Don't tell him anything else, Ewell," Mrs. Brown said.

"I'm sorry, Mrs. Brown," Ewell apologized.

"Shut up," the robber man told them. "Both of you."

For a minute we all held our breath. It seemed like the man might shoot us all or something. He acted really nervous, scared. I tried not to think about that big, black .45.

"Does it?" the guy asked Ewell again.

"Does it what?" Ewell said.

"Does it have a key, you dumb shit."

"T...t..the truck?"

"No," the man said. "The moon. You're really stupid, boy."

"It don't need one," Ewell at last got out. "It's got a floorboard starter."

"None of you moves till we're gone, hear me?" The man swung that .45 at each of us in turn.

Mrs. Brown looked like she was going to cry. Me and Ewell was quiet as church mice. Then we got lucky, I guess, because the man just stormed to the back of the store and ran outside.

As soon as he was gone, Mrs. Brown hurried back behind the counter and began checking the register to see if the man took everything. Me and Ewell ran to a window and looked outside to see what the robber man and the other guy in the car were going to do. The man that had robbed the store stopped by the other car for a minute and said something to the other guy and then jumped in the old truck. We heard the engine grinding, but it wouldn't turn over at first and we were afraid the guy was going to come back inside.

Lucky, though, he didn't. The other guy got out of the Ford and helped push the truck down the hill to the west. We heard it start and then the other guy came back, got in the sedan and took off after the truck. Me and Ewell waited a minute or two more, then ran outside to see where they went. In a couple of minutes we could see them up on the hill on Maple Street above Washington School. The truck didn't seem to be moving.

"I bet the darned thing stalled," Ewell said, almost laughing. "It dies all the time on me."

"Wow," I said. "Look."

On the hill we could see the robber get out of the truck and run back to the sedan. In no time they took off, roaring down Maple towards College. Me and Ewell hustled back towards the store.

"Hide beside the store," Ewell told me. "They might be comin' back."

"Oh, yeah."

The thought of those robbers returning to the store gave me a pretty good scare. We hurried over to the west side of the building and peered out around the edge of the building.

"There they go," Ewell exclaimed, as we saw the Ford go blasting down College heading south. They were really going fast.

When we went back into the store, Mrs. Brown was all upset. She hollered at Ewell to go tell the police and to look for Mr. Brown on the square.

I finally remembered why I had come to the store in the first place. Mrs. Brown was too nervous and stuff to wait on me, though so Ewell got my food real fast while I found the quarters I'd hid. Then he just flew out of the store on his way downtown to find Mr. Brown.

Mrs. Brown didn't seem to notice I was in the store, so I just left my Coca-Cola half full and ran out of there, headed back home to tell Aunt Margaret about what had happened.

My folks and Uncle Charley were home by then, and all the grownups acted real interested in my story of the robbery. Aunt Margaret asked if I was still interested in seeing the Edward G. Robinson gangster movie but I told her I had probably had enough experience with criminals for one day. Everyone laughed and my dad tousled my hair like he used to when I was a little boy.

We didn't come into town for another week or so after the robbery, and when we did Uncle Charley said that I was a part of history. I had witnessed a robbery by the famous Barrow Gang. He showed me the local newspaper stories about it and they said it had been Clyde and Buck Barrow themselves that robbed Brown's Grocery. Later that same day, after me and Ewell had watched them race away in their Ford sedan, they had killed a constable down Alma way, near Fort Smith.

Uncle Charley said he doubted it was Clyde, because he'd heard Clyde never, ever, left Bonnie Parker's side. My daddy said they were rotten cowards for shooting that constable, and for stealing such a piddling amount from the Brown's. I told them about the robber man stealing Ewell's thirty-five cents, and how I hid my quarters in behind the cans of vegetables. The two men shook their heads about that and then daddy said that was real smart of me. Uncle Charley told us how he read in the Kansas City paper one time that even other crooks didn't think much of these Barrows.

"Heck," Uncle Charley said. "The paper wrote that John Dillinger himself thought Bonnie and Clyde was nothing hardly at all. Amateurs they were. It said old Dillinger made fun of them and said 'They give bank robbing a bad name.'"

Uncle Charley and daddy got a good laugh out of that one.

I would've laughed, too, but I was there when that one robbed the store and he seemed plenty mean to me, whether he was a big shot crook or not. Besides, John Dillinger wasn't exactly anybody to look up to either, maybe. Shoot, it wasn't very long after that he got shot all to death himself.

I figured that maybe none of them gangsters, neither Pretty Boy Floyd, Baby Face Nelson, John Dillinger, or even Bonnie and Clyde and their gang, was such hot patootas as the papers made them out to be.

Either way, the Brown's Grocery robbery was enough excitement for me to last a lifetime. It pretty much soured me on gangster movies for quite a while. And if I had been a part of history like Uncle Charley said I was, well, I reckoned that was all of it that I needed to be in. I would be plenty content to be a regular guy living a regular life. I could never see no truck in going around robbing banks and either getting thrown in jail or shot dead. Didn't make no sense to me at all. It never did and it never will.

Police Action: October 17, 1951

Artillery fire echoed through the foggy morning air. At one end of a large Chinese bunker it had taken his unit three bloody days to capture, Johnny D. Waters watched distant puffs of smoke rise along the rocky Korean hillside. There was a short gap between first sight of smoke and the crashing rumble of the shell-spewing enemy cannons.

Johnny's platoon, depleted and weary from ten days of steady, bitter fighting, was from I Company, Third Battalion, Eighth Cavalry Regiment, First Cavalry Division, I Corps, Eighth Army—or simply, the Third of the Eighth. Only eight men remained from the platoon's maximum strength of fifteen.

The 3rd of the 8th had been sent into the hills along the western front after the latest peace talks broke off in Kaesong. Operation Commando, though short-lived and designed to force the Chinese back to the peace table, produced heavy casualties on both sides of the combat lines.

"We are prepared to strike, and strike hard," General Ridgway pronounced harshly from Tokyo just two weeks before. "The Eighth Army is not planning to sit idly by while the communists string out negotiations for another long period."

General Ridgway's strategy, unknown to the grunts who fought it on the ground, proved effective. The high command believed they were close to bringing the communist advances to a permanent standstill.

"It's comin' closer, Johnny D.," a young cigarette-smoking soldier sighed.

"Scares the hell out of me," another, still younger, soldier added.

"Hell, Stanley," the smoker said. "You're scared of your own shadow. You ain't seen nothin' yet. You ain't been here long enough."

"Take it easy, Ed," Johnny said. "We was just as scared ourselves."

"Were you really, Johnny?" Stanley asked hopefully.

"Sure, buddy," Johnny said. "Ed talks big but we were scared to death. Weren't we, Ed?"

"Hmph," Ed snorted. He snuffed out his cigarette and immediately lit another one.

"What was it like, you guys?" Stanley asked.

"It wadn't a damn peace camp, I'll tell you that," Ed sneered.

"I liked it back down at the peace camp," Stanley said wistfully.

"Ain't good to talk about," Johnny said. "Better leave it be."

Suddenly, there was a tremendous explosion nearby and the three soldiers ducked below the edge of the bunker. A light, chill wind passed over them. Johnny folded his arms across his chest, leaning his M-1 rifle against the side of the bunker.

"Jesus, that felt cold," he said.

"I can't hardly stand it," Stanley said anxiously.

"Get used to it," Ed grumbled. "We ain't even close to winter yet. Geez."

Johnny looked at him. Ed just shrugged his shoulders. Stanley peered over the edge of the bunker, then ducked back down.

"You guys afraid of dyin'?" He looked at Johnny.

"Shut up, stupid," Ed barked. "Didn't you hear nothin' John D. said?"

"Just be quiet, Stanley," Johnny said. "Keep it to yourself."

"Okay, Johnny," Stanley said. He looked down the bunker and saw the platoon sergeant moving quickly towards them.

"Knock off the jabberin'," the sergeant commanded as he got closer. "And get your weapons ready. The enemy's comin' up behind that artillery fire and things are going to get a little excitin' around here. You girls be prepared."

"Very funny," Ed said, when the sergeant was out of earshot. Stanley huddled against the back of the bunker, his rifle lying beside him. Ed nodded to Johnny.

"Let him be," Johnny said quietly. Ed shook his head and looked away.

The artillery fire, having reached a peak, broke off. They could smell the smoke in the air. The sun brightened the rust brown hillsides, but gave no warmth.

For Johnny D., the next quarter of an hour might have been an eternity, or the blinking of an eye. The enemy advance paused. The GIs caught their breath, smoked a cigarette, checked weapons and ammo, grabbed a quick bite. Then it began again. In an instant it seemed, the hazy foothills below were filled with charging, yelling enemy soldiers.

"Damn," the sergeant cursed. He sprang up in front of the line and ran back and forth like a madman. "Check your weapons. Fix bayonets. Hold your fire till I tell you to, Goddamn it, you hear me?"

All the men did hear, but they looked past the him to the field below. It seemed to stretch to infinity with enemy troops.

"Looks as many as Hill 334," Johnny called out to Ed.

"334, hell," Ed growled. "This is gonna make ever thing we seen before look like a cake walk."

"What's this one?" Stanley asked. "What's its number?"

"This country ain't nothin' but hills and mountains," Johnny said under his breath. "Never seen nothin' like it."

"This here is Hill 346, rookie," Ed growled at Stanley. "If that means shit to ya."

"Oh, God," Stanley moaned. He jumped involuntarily as small arms fire—not at the sergeant's order—exploded from all along the ridge on which their unit had dug in.

The sergeant's renewed cursing was lost amid the noise and the smoke. The air filled with the tinkle of spent casings hitting the ground and the deathly metallic whispers of enemy fire. Johnny and Ed stood side by side, firing without pause at the mass of charging troops.

"We're gettin' 'em," Ed yelled through clenched teeth. "Look, look."

Stanley stood to Ed's left, hands frozen on his rifle. Neither Ed nor Johnny had time to notice.

"Damn it," Johnny said. "Damn them."

The exchange continued for a few moments, then died down as the enemy charge slowed.

"Fix bayonets," the sergeant bellowed during the lull. "Get your Goddamn knives ready now, you dumb bastards."

With a frightening clamor, the assault began again. Though the air was fall cool, Johnny felt sweat pop out all over his body. He loaded and emptied his rifle as fast as he could, but it seemed to make no difference. The enemy continued to come. They were close enough now that he could see the color of their uniforms.

Then slowly, imperceptibly, and against Johnny's will, a notion began to work its way into his consciousness. He tried to resist, but could not. The notion was the imminence of his own death. It made the battle scene before him slow, and he saw into a tunnel of clarity that extended only directly before him. His peripheral vision noted but filtered out the death of Stanley, who fell beside Ed with a shattered skull—the bullet-smashed brain exposed carelessly to the crisp air.

Johnny continued to fire at the enemy, whose faces he could now see. All the while he struggled to keep extraneous thoughts from his mind. He could not help but think of his desert home, his father and mother, and the pretty brown-skinned girl perhaps waiting there still. He forced air into his burning lungs, felt desperately the need to live, and how terrible it was that he would never again feel the heat of the summer sun or the warm winds of fall and spring.

Johnny pulled the trigger on his rifle until he realized it was no longer firing. Then he swung the rifle up, bayonet first, in anticipation of the final charge. He felt, but did not see, Ed's bullet-riddled body fall beside him.

As the enemy swept over the bunker, Johnny stood fast, sweat pouring down his dirt-stained face. The first bullet struck him squarely in the forehead; he was instantly dead. He did not feel the half dozen other rounds penetrate his flesh, nor the tentative, prying bayonet forced into his body just below the ribs.

The cold sun shone down brilliantly over the battleground. The assault at last was over. Across the cluttered field a brisk breeze lifted the remaining wisps of smoke and sent them floating into the empty sky. It was not yet one o'clock. The day was just half gone.

Waiting for Jesus

"Jesus Christ," Reverend Polk intoned, "died for our sins. He gave his mortal life on the bloody cross of Calvary that we might have eternal life. He is the light, the way, the salvation."

"Amen," a voice fervently declaimed.

"In my Father's house there are many mansions, if it were not so I would have told you. He is a great and merciful God. Praise the Lord."

"Praise the Lord," several parishioners cried out.

"Oh, brethren, many are the snares and temptations of this earth. But if we heed Jesus we may live righteously and say as our Lord did—Get thee hence, Satan! In Matthew Seven, verses seven and eight, Jesus says Ask and it shall be given you, seek and ye shall find, knock and it shall be opened unto you. For every one that asketh receiveth, and he that seeketh findeth, and to him that knocketh it shall be opened."

"Hallelujah," a parishioner called out. There was a chorus of supporting hallelujahs.

"But, oh, brothers and sisters, there are traps in this world we may not even realize. Even as I speak, there arises a new demon to test the will of God and man. It is the hateful specter of international terrorism. It threatens the very foundation of our Christian society. These mindless killers would destroy our faith, take our sons and daughters from us, and enslave us all under the yoke of tyranny."

"Amen," the congregation agreed.

"But there is still hope. There will always be hope. Jesus Christ gave us that hope on Calvary. The Lord God loved us so well, in all our sinfulness, that He gave His only begotten Son. What a glorious thing." The reverend paused briefly.

"And how can we make ourselves worthy of such a sacrifice?" he then asked. "What must we do to live in the eternal light of His love? There's only one way. Each of us must accept Jesus Christ as our personal savior. Turn over our lives to Him. Be a witness to the greatness and compassion of God.

"Yes, friends, I ask each of you this morning to let Jesus Christ come into your heart. If you are already saved then I only ask you reaffirm your faith, strengthen your salvation here this morning in hymn, worship, and prayer.

"But if there are any of you who have slipped from the path of righteousness or have not accepted Jesus as your personal savior then step forward, come and kneel before the altar and be saved. Accept Jesus Christ as the salvation of your mortal soul. Come forward now. Come forward now."

As the Reverend ended his plea, soft organ music filled the room. In a moment there was another sound, a low rustling, and then one at a time several people came up to kneel before the altar to accept Jesus Christ as their personal savior. Frank Mason was among them.

Frank burned inside, aflame with the idea of being saved by the mysterious power of Jesus. Head bowed, he concentrated all his power on accepting Christ into his heart.

"Oh, Lord," Reverend Polk prayed. "Guide us unto the path of righteousness. Send us your eternal blessing of salvation through your son, Jesus Christ, our Lord and Savior."

The small group before the altar concentrated on finding salvation. They squinted their eyes and swayed lightly from the intensity of their effort. Frank worked and worked to be saved but he could not feel anything changing. A couple of people near him fell back in a faint. Frank assumed they had been saved.

He concentrated harder, imagining his heart had a door—just as the cover of his two-page Sunday School program showed—and Jesus was waiting outside, waiting for Frank to open that door and receive Him physically into his heart. It was a reassuring image and Frank worked to make it become a metaphysical reality. He wanted desperately to be saved. He flung the mental door to his heart wide open.

"Oh, Jesus," he prayed. "Please save me, please. I want to be saved."

Frank waited, waited for the flood of warmth he expected when Jesus would enter his body—his soul—but nothing happened. Looking over at the others while Reverend Polk's prayer droned on, Frank could see that they had all been saved. It was working for them, why not for him?

He squinted harder and tried again and again to let Jesus come into his heart. He begged Jesus, pleaded with him, yet as Reverend Polk's prayer ended so did Frank's hope. Jesus was not there, not in Frank's heart. Something was wrong, nothing had happened at all, nothing.

Disappointed and afraid the others would know that he had not been saved, Frank rose with them to receive the Reverend's blessing. He could not understand why his efforts to welcome the Prince of Peace into his heart had failed. He kept his head bowed low as Reverend Polk concluded a final prayer welcoming the saved sheep into the fold of the blessed Shepherd of men.

Standing before the Reverend, Frank reckoned something in him had stopped Jesus from coming in. Echoing the rhetoric from the only pulpits he'd seen, he felt keenly the loss of his soul. He must be a bad person, he reasoned, else Jesus would have come into him like he did those other people. That the Savior of all mankind had not come into his heart was proof of Frank's own sinfulness and damnation.

But what troubled him most was that at the crucial moment when he had most prepared himself for Christ, at the most significant of moments, he had felt nothing. Nothing had happened at all, nothing. It made him miserable. He lowered his eyes and stared at the floor, the only thing lower than himself.

The services concluded, Frank drifted forlornly out the door with the crowd of worshippers. They smiled and chatted in social groups outside the church, none noticing the boy who weaved his way among them. Frank was glad he was invisible to the adults. He knew he was worse than all of them combined.

Jesus had not chosen to bless him with His holy presence and Frank knew that meant he was damned forever. He had heard preachers say as much many times before. Slowly winding his way towards his home only a few short blocks from the church, Frank seldom looked up as he walked. He was far too self-absorbed, too concerned—he mourned greatly for the loss of his ten-year-old soul.

Ozark Beats

I first saw him coming up the sidewalk past the city ice plant. He didn't see us until he reached the corner, at the intersection of West and Dickson. I swear his eyes got so big you would have thought they'd pop out of his head. I nudged Bernie to check the kid out but he wasn't very interested and just grunted.

I thought the little guy was kind of cute, really, and I could tell he was fascinated by us. He meant no harm staring. We were probably something he'd never seen before. He was intrigued, that's all.

"He's like all of them around here," Bernie growled as we turned up Dickson towards the university. "He'll grow up to be just another inbred cracker yelling at people like us."

"Oh, Bernie, they aren't all like that. And they're not crackers here, that's Georgia."

"Hmph," Bernie grumbled.

"Remember that old country couple when the car broke down?" I reminded him. "They were really nice to us."

The boy was walking along the other side of the street, keeping up with us but pretending like he wasn't, and like he wasn't watching us for all he was worth. I smiled at him but he turned his head away really fast. That tickled me.

"Don't encourage him," Bernie said, "these idiots will think we're going to reefer him to death or something."

"Bernie, you're completely neurotic," I laughed. "You've got to stop smoking before we go out down here. It's not like home, nobody notices us there."

"That's for sure," he sighed, "I can walk around the city anywhere and there's no damned Okie bugging me."

"They're Arkies, and besides we don't have to stay. We can go home any time we want."

"Don't start that again," Bernie said all frustrated, his hands whipping so wild in the air the little kid across the street stopped in his tracks and watched us with his mouth wide open. "Just don't do it, man. It ain't cool. You dig? I came down here to be with the people and to get some material to write about. I ain't going till then, dig?"

"I dig."

I thought what a silly thing it was to leave New York, where we had friends and nobody called us names and go to some out of the way southern town to study people that we—at least Bernie anyway—couldn't stand for a second. All this for art, I thought. What a load of baloney.

I smiled over at the little boy again and thought I saw a smile flicker on his face. He might even have been digging me, the little fart. Maybe he was small for his age or something and was kind of getting off on a strange-looking chick. That was okay, too. Didn't bother me.

"Come on," Bernie mumbled in that way of his I call "New York Wimpy" when I'm teasing him. "Let's get on to a cafe and eat, we got a lot of work in the library tonight and I wanna write some later, okay?"

"Okay," I said, sneaking another peek at our small shadow. "Let's go."

When we turned onto Arkansas Avenue headed for Joe's Shoat Diner, a real life greasy spoon with great food up past the north side of campus, I saw the boy for the last time. He had a funny look in his eyes, I thought, like he was unhappy we weren't going his way anymore. I gave him a quick wink and a wave but he acted like he didn't see me. He was a cute kid and I liked the way he was interested in us. It made you think all the people down here weren't the same, that maybe some of them might be something different than a dumb hick someday.

• • •

Boy was I surprised when I saw them right down there on Dickson and West. Jeez, right in the middle of town, or sort of, at least real near the university anyway. I couldn't wait to tell Troy and the other guys. I bet they never seen any of them. I never noticed them till I was nearly at the corner past the ice plant and then I stood there a second until they turned up Dickson and headed towards the university. I had heard of them or something but I hadn't seen any of them.

The woman was all dressed in black just like the man except that she didn't have one of those little caps or hats like he was wearing, like you see on French painters in books sometimes. She was really kinda pretty and I would've liked to have seen her boobs, but I just walked up Dickson like I was heading that way and acted like I didn't see them or anything. Every now and then they acted like they saw me watching but I quick turned away so I wouldn't be noticed.

The guy she was with was pretty weird. I mean, he had that little French painter's hat and was wearing dark sunglasses even though it wasn't that bright. He acted kinda huffy towards her and he for sure never looked over at me. He had a mustache and his beard was growing out, which is weird for here, and he walked funny, kinda like he was bopping along or something like that. You could tell just looking at him that he wasn't from around here. He must have been from up north, or back east, but I couldn't tell really, all I knew is that he wasn't from this area.

But now the girl, she was okay. She was all the stuff he was but she was neat looking, too. Her black sweater made her push out real tight-like in the front and it looked real good. Her pants were good and tight, too, and made her bottom stick out a little, though not too much. I looked a couple of times at that. She kept looking at me and she smiled every time and once I kinda smiled back but it was pretty embarrassing and I looked away real fast.

They were real different and I liked that, in a funny sort of way. Even the guy, 'cause I figured it must be something to be that weird in a little town like this. I hadn't seen anybody else be it. I wondered who they were and where they really came from. I knew for a certainty that they were going to the university.

Boy, they were something unusual alright, and that was pretty darn neat. And the girl, kinda being nice looking and all was pretty cool. She seemed real calm about everything, just walking along checking everything out and not letting anything bug her. I felt that way when she would smile at me. You could tell she was a nice person. I shouldn't've thought dirty things about her but I couldn't help it. She was real pretty.

Right past the UArk Theatre, they turned on Arkansas Avenue and that's when I had to stop following them. The guy just went on but the woman turned back and looked at me again. She smiled real nice and waved. I sorta smiled back I guess and then stopped and watched them go up the street until they disappeared.

I felt kinda bad when they went out of sight and lonely, like when you look up in the sky and see a plane going over and you wonder who's on board and where it's going. Kind of a funny sadness though, where you feel good and bad at the same time. It's hard to say, I don't know.

Anyway, that was the way I felt and since I didn't have to go home right away I walked back to the UArk and stood out front for a few minutes looking at the preview pictures. After a little bit I took off down University Street past the cemetery and headed home in a kind of roundabout way.

All the way back I thought about those two people I'd seen. For the longest time I could picture them in my mind real good. They were different, unusual. After a while, though, I couldn't see them so clear in my mind's eye and their memory kinda faded over the years. But it never left me completely. Now and again I wonder about them; wonder where they went, what happened to them, who they became. Yeah, I still wonder about them—sometimes.

Still Life:

Girl On Snowy Night

The boy emptied the hot silverware from the big dishwasher tray into tall, fluted metal cups, jamming each until it was completely full. He set the cups of silverware next to several stacks of dishes at one side of his cleaning area, then rinsed out two deep tubs where he had already done the odious chore of cleaning pots and pans. Watching the last of the soapy water swirl down the drain, the boy sighed and did his best to dry his hands on a mostly-wet towel.

Now fourteen, the boy had been washing dishes since he was twelve. His first job was at the local bus station cleaning glasses, dishes, and smaller pans for the travelers who strayed through town on their way to bigger, unknown places. The boy hated the restaurant boss, disliked the travelers, and loathed the hot humid job of dishwasher. But it was what he did, his only skill.

After the bus station, he moved to his present job at a drive-in restaurant, a hot college spot near campus. Here he worked four to midnight on Friday and Saturday nights, four to eight on Sunday so that he could ostensibly do his homework before the next school week began.

Sometimes after work on Sunday nights, he liked to clear his head from the accumulated hubbub of work by taking a short walk in the evening air. He would go up through the university and loop back around to go home, back to the small house where his family lived just a couple of short blocks behind the drive-in.

One cold Sunday evening in January with a light wind blowing a light snow around, the boy left work and headed down the street towards the campus. He walked along slowly, shoes squeaking in the accumulating snow. He saw himself in the windows of the newsstand where he read all the sports magazines and, surreptitiously, the girlie magazines. Pulling the collar of his old coat tighter against his neck with one hand, he tried to comb down a small cowlick in his hair with the other.

Walking on, he went past the railroad station—now out of use—and over the tracks he often took in getting around town. The street climbed up then, past a drug store with a candy and cigar machine out front where he and his buddies bought the nausea-producing smokes they experimented with off and on.

Further up there was a Piggly Wiggly store set well back off the street and then the old bowling alley. Across from the bowling lanes was the college theatre where, a few years back, the boy had seen Jimmy Stewart in *Winchester 73*.

He turned right on the street just below the elevated grounds of the university campus where he went as often as he could. He liked to walk its sidewalks filled with the engraved names of graduates from years gone by, tried to imagine what they had been like and who they had become. The campus was always beautiful to him with its huge oak and maple trees, its well-kept grounds and its wonderful centerpiece, Old Main. In that two-towered brick building was his favorite place almost in the whole world—the museum, with its reconstructed Mastodon skeleton, its Civil War exhibits, and one peculiar room full of intoxicating, multi-colored glass bottles and vases.

Near the center of the campus grounds were a set of steps leading up to Old Main and the boy headed for those. The wind had nearly died down and snow fell softly though steadily. There was a street lamp near the steps and it shone down on the sidewalk like a cool white spotlight.

The boy paused at the curb to check for cars and then walked out to a tree-lined median that divided the road. He had to wait a moment on the median as a south-bound car drove slowly by, its tires crunching the snow beneath.

When the car passed, its glaring lights no longer blocking the boy's vision, he stepped out into the street and slowly made his way to the opposite curb. As he reached the other sidewalk, he looked over at the stairs beneath the street lamp.

And there she was.

There she was, standing on the sidewalk in front of the steps in the snow under the light. The boy had not seen where she came from. She was just suddenly there. A young coed framed in the halo-light of the street lamp. The boy stopped in place.

In that brief moment, as the young woman adjusted her gloves in the night air, looking up the street away from the boy, he saw her as a lustrous, motionless, still life. A pretty young woman in a pretty winter coat.

Her hair appeared to be light brown and her face, in profile, was smooth and finely shaped, with prominent cheekbones and a soft, rounded chin. The boy absorbed her grace and beauty in stunned awe.

From the scarf she wore around her neck to her stylish winter boots, she was—though probably no more than 21 years old—the essence of a grown, mature woman, beautiful and in her prime. Her face glowed in the light. Her cheeks were flushed from the cold and from a natural, youthful vigor. Her skin was so white in the light, so soft and smooth, it caused the boy to catch his breath. She seemed to carry in her being a pleasant calmness, a self-assuredness that in this cold, bright moment under the street light made her the most wonderful thing the boy had ever seen in his life.

She was—in a flash of powerful feeling, one that stirred within the boy a simultaneous mixture of emotional longing, lust, purity of motive, and love—a vision of ultimate desire, a desire of great depth, a desire unobtainable.

The boy ached with a melancholy and an exhilaration that commingled in his mind and heart. He wanted the girl, loved her without knowing her, wanted to know about her—where she came from, where she would go, what her life would be like. And then, after waiting for another car to go by, she crossed the street.

He passed less than ten feet below her on the sidewalk but she never saw him. He paused at the base of the steps leading up to the campus and looked back, watched her until she disappeared into the night.

She was gone.

Gone back to whatever world in which she lived. A world, perhaps, of sororities and fraternities, of money and nice homes, of comfort and ease. The boy, unfamiliar with such a world, huddled in his coat, and without looking back walked on past the campus and then doubled back towards the dark little house where he lived.

The snow began to fall heavier then and the boy hurried on, hurried away from the bright beauty of the campus there on the hill above town, on the hill that seemed now so far above him, so far from where he lived just a few short blocks away, far from his own small home.

Time Pieces:

Something Lost — A Night of Stars

A Night of Stars

"Hurry up with that jug," Kenny Dornan said. "Or give it back if you ain't gonna drink any."

Jim Finerty took a quick sip and handed the quart bottle back to his friend. He shivered a little as the cold liquid coursed through his system.

With Jim only a week away from a move out of the Ozarks to the unknown world of Southern California, the two old friends shared a final illegal quart of beer. Kenny believed it was the only way to give his lifelong buddy a proper send-off. For the time being, Jim was mostly interested in Kenny's exploits with girls, an area in which Jim was at yet totally deficient.

"What about you and Brenda the other night? he asked. "Did you touch her boobies, really? Did you?"

"Natch." Kenny said nonchalantly.

"What'd they feel like?"

"Good. Good and firm. Warm. Soft, too."

"Oooh."

"I had her naked from the waist up."

"No kiddin'?"

"No kiddin'."

Jim tried to picture that. It made him tingle to imagine Brenda's beautiful breasts, naked and waiting to be touched. He let out a big sigh.

For several minutes he and Kenny were silent, Kenny holding the beer. Jim looked up at the star-filled sky, then peered down the hill at the vague outline of the university football stadium. It loomed in the darkness like some frozen, monolithic being. He felt a funny mood slip over him and tried vainly to think of Brenda Lowery's breasts. He couldn't maintain the needed concentration.

"Here." Kenny offered Jim the beer. Jim squinted to see his friend in the dark. "Here, take it. Take a swig."

"Yeah."

Jim took a drink, bigger than he intended, and almost coughed as his mouth and throat filled with the bitter liquid. He grimaced and handed the bottle back to Kenny.

"Good, huh?"

"Yeah," Jim whispered. "Great."

"You suppose there's life up there, somewhere?" Kenny said after a bit. "You know, other beings?"

"What'd you say that for?" Jim asked.

"Huh?"

"How come?"

"I don't know. Just wonderin'. It seems to me like there'd have to be, you know. Look up there at all the stars. Look at that."

Jim saw that the sky hung down over them like a huge light-dotted black cover. There was something scary about it, though he couldn't say what.

"Do you think there's anything?" Kenny asked again. He handed Jim the beer.

"No. I knew…. I don't know. Maybe. Yes. Maybe," Jim muttered.

He glanced again at the far off stars. They seemed cold. Scary somehow. The night sky made him feel like he was in some kind of tunnel. He gripped the beer bottle tightly in his hand.

"Do you believe in God?" he heard himself ask Kenny.

"Sure, don't you?"

Jim looked up again. There were so many stars. In a powerful rush he felt their magnitude and the immeasurable immensity of the universe.

"Oh, my God," he said.

"What?" Kenny said. "What did you say?"

"Is there a God? I mean, how can there be? Something would have had to have made Him, too, wouldn't it? There can't be one. It would have had to go on forever like that. It couldn't happen."

"God always was and always will be, damn it," Kenny said. "Didn't you learn anything in Sunday School?"

"But where'd He come from? Something can't come from nothing. Did He make Himself?"

"I don't know, jeez."

"Don't you think about these things?"

"No. I don't. I got better things to think about, like girls."

"Do you think things go on forever?"

"Of course."

"They don't end?"

"How could they?"

"How can they? Everything ends. Stops. Dies."

"Not in eternal life."

"Even that has to end. Nothing can last forever. It must end. Oh, Jesus."

"Say, man," Kenny said. "What's buggin' you anyway?"

"It don't make no sense," Jim said. "How can anything exist? It's all gonna end. Everything. It had to start and it has to end. But...none of it's possible. Jesus Christ."

He felt the cosmic inevitability of the end of all things, and the message seemed to belong to and be transmitted by the icy stars twinkling in the vast blackness overhead. When he looked up yet again it was not the lights of a hopeful existence that he saw, but the malevolent signaling of an indifferent, inhumane force. It waited only for the opportunity to engulf him in its existence-ending void. Mortality was a trap.

"Jesus, I can't escape. Nothing's possible. It just can't be."

"Goddamn it, Jim," Kenny said. "Knock it off. You're givin' me the willies with all this shit. You dumbass, give the bottle here."

"Nothing."

"Oh, shut up," Kenny said. He jerked the bottle out of Jim's hand. "What's the matter with you anyway? You must be getting all scared about moving away or something."

"You don't understand. Nothing. Nothing can't be nothing. Or something. It's not possible."

"Oh, shit," Kenny laughed. "Get serious." He stepped back away into the dark with what was left of the beer. "You're just being dumb now. I thought you wanted to talk about girls. Cripes."

Jim stayed motionless for several minutes. He was different than he had been just a quarter of an hour before. His head buzzed and all he wanted was to be free of the logic he felt he could never again escape.

Nothing made sense anymore. Existence itself seemed totally illogical. It was like a cosmic trap door you fell through. Only it was not funny. He felt trapped. Bound. He hadn't asked for any of it, no one had. He shuddered to think of it. He was consumed by it.

Then just as he began to feel it would never end, the mood passed of its own volition. He felt a warmth inside, a sense of relief. His spirits began to lift. He felt exhausted and sat down weakly on the wet grass. This strange moment, so unexpected, so outside his prior experience, had passed. It had left him, gone for the time being.

Daring to look up again, he gazed at the panoply of stars above him. They didn't seem quite so cold now. They had taken on a little of their former luster. But not all. Something had been lost. Something he had always felt to be true about them. Something that would never be there again. Something he would never get back.

A Terrible Sound

Jim wiped the sweat from his forehead and leaned forward slowly to pull his soaked t-shirt away from the back of his chair.

"Ugh," he grunted.

The creaky swamp cooler, mounted ineffectually in the window that faced the afternoon desert sun, barely cooled even a small area of the tiny living room. The radio blared out "A Quarter to Three" and Jim sweated. And looked out the window at the cool-looking white adobe house on the other side of the street.

He was hoping to see Bonnie Sears. For most of the month he and his mother had lived in the hot little cracker box across from Bonnie, Jim had settled for occasional voyeuristic glimpses of the tall, well-developed girl watering the lawn or leaving on some chore for her mother. Waiting for peeks at Bonnie and listening non-stop to the Top 40 was all Jim did in those early tedious days in California.

One of his diversions, as he sat alone in the house sweating, was to recall his trip from his former home in the Ozarks to California. He vividly pictured himself leaving. He climbed aboard a Trailways bus trying to act grown-up, on this his first long trip alone, but he knew he must have looked like the world's biggest country bumpkin. All the way to Dallas he sat alone, feeling awkwardly stupid, as if his naiveté was so transparent it may as well have been pinned to the bill of the worn out Yankees baseball cap he wore.

He remembered certain details of the trip. Like the beauty queen who got on the bus in some one-horse town west of Dallas and sat beside him until a rest stop in another small town after which he had timidly let an older Mexican man take the girl's seat. The look she had given him left him feeling miserable for hundreds of miles.

After the Mexican man got off, he was replaced by a young California guy who only seemed interested in talking about something called party-partying—an activity Jim was grateful not to have to admit to anyone he knew nothing about. At some hole in the wall meal stop, Mr. Party-Party missed getting back on the bus and Jim celebrated that quirk of time and fate for many pleasantly quiet miles.

El Paso, however, was the worst of all. During a long layover, Jim bought a fancy Texas ashtray for his California aunt and sat alone on a bench, his small traveling bag next to him.

After a while, an amiable, cleanly dressed man in his mid-forties sat down and struck up a conversation. Shortly, the man excused himself to go to the restroom and asked Jim to watch his suitcase. Jim obliged and when the man returned he asked the favor in return.

His own business done, Jim returned to find the friendly man gone. He looked all over the station but neither the man nor the bag was in sight. Eventually he found the bag in a trash can—empty, of course, except for a pack of flat bubble gum and baseball cards he'd picked up before he left home. The ashtray in the shape of Texas was gone.

"Damn," he said himself, sheepishly putting the bag under his arm and stalking back to a bench. "Damn."

He was glad nobody he knew had been around to see what

a fool he was. His face had burned with shame and the incident preyed upon him the rest of the way into New Mexico and Arizona. He debated telling his mother about the incident, but between Yuma and El Centro, his destination, he decided against it, choosing to swallow the humiliation and loss of the ashtray stoically. He figured he'd try to buy his aunt something else. He didn't know whether she smoked or not anyway.

Now, less than a month later, sitting by himself in the stifling ninety-plus degree heat of his living room, the memory of that first big bus ride seemed peculiar to him. Real enough, yet somehow bizarre, off-the-wall, oddly distant—distant as everything seemed to be this oppressive summer.

Sometime after the move, Jim developed a singular obsession. Without warning, an inexplicable, smothering, and nearly debilitating sense of death, nothingness, and the logical inevitability of both would explode into his consciousness with such intensity that he would feel he was going to cease to exist—on the spot, at that precise moment.

These explosions came in powerful rushes, unexpectedly, with almost no warning. They were preceded by an inner sound so loud it was as if a freight train bore down on him from somewhere inside his own head.

The first episode came on a blazing afternoon like today, when he stood up, pulling his sweat-sticky t-shirt away from his body, to take the few steps into the kitchen for a cold bottle of Coke. Popping the lid off with a church key, he took a drink and started back towards the living room. Suddenly it started, a peculiar buzzing sound—now so familiar to him—in his ears, coming slowly, softly at first, then sweeping through his head with a roaring, deafening blast.

"No," he cried, barely getting his pop onto a nearby table before covering his ears with his hands. "No."

Instantly, his vision was funneled, tinted yellow, the rest of the world blocked out by the overpowering assault on his senses. The sound was followed by a horrendous sense that existence itself was completely, totally illogical, impossible.

His head buzzed and he battled to free himself from this unwilled fixation on the absurd unreality yet simultaneous inevitability of both living and dying. None of this can be, he thought in his confusion, it's impossible. Nothing could always have been and always exist. It has to start. It has to end. Even eternity. Nothing can last forever. It has to all go to nothingness. Blackness.

He stood, frozen, unaware of anything outside himself, stomach cramping, cold, stinging sweat forming on his face, for how long he didn't know. The episode might have lasted only two or three minutes, perhaps less.

Then, as unexpectedly as it started, it began to lift. He came back to the world around him, slowly. He felt the first waves of a great surge of well-being and relief that always followed these experiences. Grabbing his warming soda, he stumbled back into the living room and slumped down in front of the radio, which incongruously blared "Raindrops" into the hot air blown uselessly around by the swamp cooler.

"Damn," he had said out loud, the moment fading quickly. "Jesus, what is that? What is happening?"

That was the first one. They were a regular part of his life now, occurring frequently. The episodes left him feeling tired, moody and withdrawn, always steeling himself for the next one. Another side effect was that he began to hate dusk, the coming of evening. He feared the coming of darkness, blackness, the unconsciousness of sleep and death, the void as he had once heard someone refer to the final loss of awareness. And all of it was represented perfectly by night.

He hated the night, hated nothingness, hated his own fear. It was like when he was a young boy and wondered where he went when he slept. Was that what death was like—eternal sleep. He couldn't understand that. He couldn't or wouldn't accept that he would permanently lose consciousness. He hated the thought, it terrified him.

What happens to the dead, he thought, where are they now? Nowhere? His mother had told him that as long as someone remembers you in some way you are still alive. That was okay but it would end when the memory did. He didn't want to be forgotten that way or like others he'd known who died. Like his grandfather, who he remembered lying on his long bed, blood emptying out of the back of his head, staining the mattress an ugly black-red.

In the snap of a finger, he thought, our lives will be over and we will be in our death beds. And it will be so quick. Fearing the direction of his thoughts, he drove the idea from his mind. All he wanted was for things to be back to normal. To be like they were before this frightening thing had started happening to him. Before the freight train sound had begun to roar in his ears and head at unpredictable, terrible moments.

He breathed deeply and stood. He walked to the window to see if Bonnie was around, but the only movement was the waves of heat rising from the road.

I'll get over this, he told himself hopefully, though doubtfully. It'll stop one of these days. Maybe it's because everything's different out here or something. That's probably it. It's because everything is so new to me.

He sat back down in front of the cooler. It was really hot, but he was feeling okay. He'd analyzed his problem without triggering it. That was some kind of success. He took a big, refreshing drink of Coke and leaned back in the chair. He had weathered a bunch of these things and you never knew when the next one would come, but at least he was okay for now. He picked up a stray copy of *Life* and calmly leafed through it. Yeah, he was all right. And the way things had been going this summer, that was as good as he could hope for.

Recollected in Tranquility

Jim inhaled deeply, holding the smoke deep in his lungs. When he breathed, nearly coughing, blue smoke escaped from his mouth and nostrils. He half-heartedly waved it back towards his face.

On the creek bank in front of him, Amy paced back and forth, trying not to look bored. The creek, maybe twelve feet across at its widest point, ran swiftly along. It was shallow, not much more than ankle deep. Jim watched her stop and listen to it run, splashing over the rocky bottom. He knew she liked the creek, imagined that it reminded her of when she was small—still innocent and full of expectations.

Amy looked over at Jim where he sat on the quilt amid the remains of their picnic, writing and smoking. She turned back to the creek. Jim understood that she prided herself on not bothering him when he wrote. He liked that about her.

Fifteen I stood there my friend, Jim wrote with a ground down Number 1 pencil, *and I sharing my first—his who knew how many—quart of beer/The grass was late spring dew wet/above the empty stadium.*

He took a drink of soda and let it coat his smoke-scratchy throat. He looked up at Amy again. She was pretending not to be bored. He watched her walk, her young, tight buttocks moving with the natural sexual rhythm of a young woman. Watching her made him ache and he sighed, a mixture of sexual release, frustration, and desire. He tried to concentrate on writing.

Here have a shot he said/Yeah drinking grimacing a throat full of bitter/Do you suppose there's life up there.

What a night, Jim remembered, the words of his poem triggering the past association. In one moment it was all gone, like a weight dropped. His siblings already gone from home before he and his mother moved away. No one to talk to. You can't tell your mother at fifteen you just lost God and church and faith. Not quite then.

And me looking up like some fool/saw stars cold far emptier than the stadium shivered/Do you think there's anything/No I said I don't know yes maybe/Scared like never before but many times since/Vision tunneled gut hurt fear frozen/God I said Oh Jesus God.

"Hey," Amy called out. Jim looked up, annoyed. "Are you done yet?" she asked, walking back towards him.

"In a minute," he said roughly.

But as she came nearer, he quickly softened. When she knelt down and kissed him, his annoyance fled.

"Listen," he said, looking into her light blue eyes. "I won't be much longer. Okay?"

"What you writing about?"

"Oh, just about a night and some stars. When I was a kid."

"Oh."

"Oh?"

"Anybody in it I know?"

"What?" he laughed.

"Is your family in it?"

"No, just a friend when I was a kid. That's all."

"Oh."

"Let me finish and we'll go back in and get a beer or something."

She rolled her eyes in mock hurt. He reached over and ran

his hand across her breasts. She slapped him playfully, then went back to the creek bank. He watched her walk away, wrote a few more short verses.

What's the matter he said/I said oh God no sense how can anything exist/What are you talking about?

"What are you talking about?" Jim remembered someone saying recently. "Killed who? Who did?"

Then a girl was crying and everybody was pissed at the president and the war and pretty soon memorial services for the four young dead students in Ohio ended up shutting down pretty much every college in the country.

They killed them flat out, he told himself. That's a fact. Just like Kennedy and King before and Jackson State right after. Like so many times before. Who knows how many more to come. And nothing ever happens about it. Nobody does anything. Nothing.

Oh Jesus it's nothing/Dumb shit give the bottle here/ Nothing/Oh shut up.

Jim looked up at a stand of trees near a bend in the creek. A light wind rustled their full leaves and he concentrated on that. It was an exercise he did often—focusing on some distant object after having read or written something up close for too long— it took the tension from your overworked eyes. Amy wasn't in sight, but he went on without looking for her.

Bowel moving skin biting hair electrifying/You don't understand nothin' can't be nothing can it's not possible/ Walked off in the dark with the bottle.

Amy came around from the side of the car and walked up behind him. He didn't turn around.

Left alone not crying scared so badly in need/with the black sky above—

And after he got pounded in a big bar fight near his school, he felt terribly alone and could only think to call his brother.

"I knew about it," Pete said.

"That's amazing. Word spread that far? How come you didn't call?"

"I figured if it was something you wanted to talk about, you would have called me."

"I'm okay, now, all I have left from the beating is a numb tooth and a scar on top of my head. Fuckin' rats. Decided they needed to punch out a dirty hippie I guess"

They both laughed. It was okay before he hung up.

"Thanks, Pete"

"Just stay out of the bars for a while," Pete told him. "We don't want you killing yourself, or somebody doing it for you. Okay?"

"Okay, I will."

"Good-bye, buddy."

"Good-bye, Pete."

Amy bent over and hugged Jim, bringing him back to the present. He pressed her hands and rubbed his cheek against one of her arms. She let him go and stood up.

Gone and gone just like that/beyond expression retelling.

Jim tossed his pad and pencil down and reached up for Amy.

"Come on," he said, pulling her down to him.

She kissed him and he reached inside her blouse to feel her firm breasts. He was already excited.

"Are you done?" she said, letting him unbutton her blouse. As it often did, his quick sexuality took her by surprise.

"Come on."

"If you're done."

"I'm done. Come here."

In a moment they lay together skin to skin from the waist up. On the edge of the quilt, the pad and pencil lay by an empty soda can and the remains of a sandwich. A light wind blew, slowly flipping the blank pages of the pad. After a decade the poem had emerged, blending past and future into the sensuous death of the present. In time, he leaned his head back and moaned.

"Finished," he said to the sky. "Done."

Revisiting the Past

"While this book's still new," Larry Driscoll said, "now's when I can get you some air time. Just don't blow it by getting out of control, okay?"

"What are you talking about?" Jim asked.

"You know what I mean," Driscoll answered. "Don't get too radical on the air. I've scheduled you on a local radio talk show. A pleasant little man is the host, so please, no hard core stuff, no raging socialism, no theories about hunting being man's attempt to wipe out his evolutionary memory or whatever. Okay? Just this once? You don't need any more bad publicity, right?"

Jim laughed. He'd had plenty of bad publicity not so long ago when a little one-horse town brought him up on indecency charges for a prior book. They wanted to charge him with sedition but even their own lawyers knew that wouldn't stick. Neither did the obscenity charge. It had sold a few books for Jim, but made his life miserable for a while, too.

"You're a real corker of an agent, Larry," he told his long-time representative. "What do I talk about, stock prices? The weather? Kiss a little you know what?"

"It's not kissing anything, Jim. It's using your head. It's practical. Look, you've had a little success, don't throw it away needlessly."

"Don't forget, it was my little success that got me into the latest scrape in the first place."

"Okay," Driscoll said, "but let's not hassle it. We're not in Podunksville, Missouri anymore and maybe with a couple of breaks you'll get the recognition you deserve."

"Isn't it pretty to think so," Jim smirked. The allusion escaped Driscoll.

Jim walked around the agent's office, looked out the window, stopped by a bookcase. Driscoll went to the center of the room. He acted like he thought it might be necessary to physically keep Jim in the room until the talk show thing was settled. Jim didn't seem interested in the discussion.

"Well, what do you know?" Jim said, picking a thin volume from the bookcase. It was a book of poetry. His own. "You ever read this, Larry?"

"What is it?" the agent asked.

"The book of poetry I wrote. You know."

"Sure," Driscoll said. "Of course. I've read all your stuff. Even your earlier things." Jim furrowed his brow. "Really, Jim, you have to trust me a little more."

Jim waved Driscoll off and began leafing through the book. Midway through he stopped. One of the poems caught his attention. It was called "Something Lost—A Night of Stars." He read to himself:

> *Fifteen I stood there my friend*
> *and I sharing my first*
> *—his who knew how many—*
> *quart of beer*
> *The grass was late spring dew wet*
> *above the empty stadium*
> *Here have a shot he said*
> *Yeah drinking grimacing a throat full of bitter*
> *Do you suppose there's life up there*
> *And me looking up like some fool*
> *saw stars cold far emptier than the stadium shivered*
> *Do you think there's anything*

No I said I don't know yes maybe
Scared like never before but many times since
Vision tunneled gut hurt fear frozen
God I said oh Jesus God
What's the matter he said
I said oh God no sense how can anything exist
What are you talking about
Oh Jesus it's nothing
Dumb shit give the bottle here
Nothing
Oh shut up
Bowel moving skin biting hair electrifying
You don't understand nothin'
can't be nothing can it's not possible
Walked off in the dark with the bottle
Left alone not crying scared so badly in need
with the black sky above –
Gone and gone just like that
beyond expression retelling.

"Good?" Driscoll asked, seeing Jim look up.

"Who knows?" Jim said. "I have my doubts."

They were quiet a moment. Jim remembered how he once said that the worst thing about writing, especially writing your own past, was that some real memories get mixed up, even replaced by the fiction or poetry. He figured it was an occupational hazard. He replaced the book on the shelf. Driscoll walked to the window behind his desk and stood looking out.

"That little trial thing shouldn't have happened, Larry, you know that, don't you?" Jim asked after a few minutes. Driscoll turned to face his client. "And you know the bad thing? I love Missouri, it's my favorite state."

"But it turned out all right," Driscoll said. "You saw. You've been able to turn it to your advantage. It's legitimized you as a writer; brought you offers. Hell, it may free you more than you can imagine."

"Or the opposite."

"Not very likely. But either way, try to look at the good side of it. Come on, you haven't had to face this alone."

"Uh."

Maybe because of the way he was it was hard for people to put up with him for very long. Maybe a little bit of him went a long way. But knowing that didn't help, in fact it made him feel all the more alone, all the more disoriented at the recent trial. He didn't like it, but he had to teach himself to practice resignation, not his long suit. Resignation, acceptance, and accommodation. Accommodation, he thought chastising himself.

He had accommodated his legal team by apologizing to any readers who might have been offended by his fiction. Accommodation in this case felt like selling out, like giving in, like giving up.

"Accommodation," he said out loud.

"Yes," Driscoll said, "that's a good word. Accommodation. Do the talk show. Move on. Go ahead with your life. That's what maturity is. That's what accommodation is." He looked to Jim for a reaction.

"To hell with accommodation," Jim said flatly.

He walked over to the door. Driscoll watched him without speaking.

"Hey, Larry, don't worry about it, okay? I'll do what has to be done, like always. I'll be the perfect little writer for you. How's that?"

"Come on, Jim, that's not fair. That's not what I want you to be. I'm looking out for you. I'm trying to help here. I believe in you, too, you know."

"I gotta go," Jim said, opening the door. "Take care of whatever you have to take care of. I'll hold up my end."

"Don't walk out now. Not like this."

"I'll see you later," Jim said, easing into the hallway.

The agent took a step towards him. Jim shut the door. He was gone. Just walked out. For several minutes Driscoll stared at the closed door.

"Well, hell," he said finally, "hell and damnation."

Field Work

We'd been pickin' tomatoes for twenty, twenty-five, minutes when I looked up and saw Mason about halfway down his second row. I was straight across from him a few rows over. He saw me and waved. I waved back and pointed up the field to where the Mexicans were already pretty near finishing their fourth row. Mason saw them and shook his head. God, them *braceros* could work. They could work you right into the ground.

"Hey, Frank," I yelled over to Mason, "get your *cúlo* in gear, *cuñado.*"

"Oh, man," he called back. "I'm dying already. My back's killing me, *cuñado.*"

He drug out the *cuñado*. That's what the workers always called us. Brother-in-law. That was *cuñado*. It comes from a Mexican joke about your sister. The *braceros* called each other that, and Esé, but they really liked to call us *cuñado*. They were just kidding us, most of them anyway. They knew we were working hard, just not as good as them. Shoot, the money was awful. A lousy dollar an hour for killing yourself in 120 degree heat. But they ate it up.

They wore blue jean jackets and long sleeve shirts and used their sweat and the wind—what little there was of it—as air conditioning. They had busted down, straw cowboy hats like we did except they would put a handkerchief or little towel underneath them so they draped down their backs like an Arab's turban or whatever. They were the hardest working men I ever seen.

Me and Mason and some of the other boys, we did this the first part of every summer but only as long as it took to find something better, easier. We usually lasted two, three weeks, a month at the most. It was too hard. Most of the time we thinned cotton with short-handled hoes. That'll kill you in this heat.

Or we weeded cotton with long-handled hoes—easier on the back but still plenty tough because of pounding the salty, hard ground. We formed up about four-thirty, a quarter to five, every morning at the *bracero* camp, loaded sleepy-eyed onto big covered flatbed trucks with some guy takin' a leak off the back and usually got to the fields by five thirty so we could get done early in the afternoon.

We did it to make a couple of bucks. They did it to support their families in Mexico. American money meant a lot. They would save it and send it home to Mexico. The only thing they spent money on was a ticket to the dinky old Mexican theatre in town, or a cheap radio or six-pack of beer.

They lived cheap. The rest they sent home. They lived for the days when a farmer had to get a tomato crop or something in fast and let 'em work by the piece. Then they could double, even triple their measly day's wages. There was no stopping them then, nobody could keep up with them.

"Jesus, I can't keep up with them," Mason called over to me. Benjy was in a row on over and he stood up and laughed.

"They should have never told them it was piece work," Benjy said.

We all laughed. It was true. Christ, they were turning in crates of tomatoes so fast it made your head swim.

"Say," Mason said. "Let's go to the truck and get a drink at the end of this row. What do you say?"

"You got a crate load?" Benjy asked.

"About," Mason said. "How about you?"

"Pretty close," Benjy said.

"Me too," I said.

After our drink, we kept on and it kept on gettin' hotter and hotter. You figure it was clearing 110 by lunch time and well on its way to 115 or more. That's the way the fields were during summer. It was like an oven in the valley and it felt like the heat hit you right around your nose so your whole head was baking. No matter what you did, it was just flat hot. But that didn't stop us or the *braceros* from eating. When it was lunchtime, we ate.

The farmers always gave you a half hour for lunch and they fed you. Every day it was the same thing: beans, tortillas, and hot peppers. If you wanted something besides water you had to bring it yourself. But the food was pretty good, at least it filled you up. The beans were wrapped in soft, warm tortillas and we'd scarf up three or four of them and maybe a Coke if somebody brought it and it didn't get swiped.

Sometimes it was a kick to watch the Mexicans eat *jalapeños*. Each guy would down maybe half a jar by himself for lunch. They looked real good through the clear glass and when they ate them. But, Jesus, those peppers would kill you. Your heart would pound and sweat would pop out all over you. You'd be drinking water for an hour if you bit straight into one.

In the afternoon, after we ate, we worked slower and by around one-thirty we'd had it. We wanted three-thirty to come so we could get the hell out of that sun and lay around in our nice cool houses. Some of the *braceros* slowed up in the afternoon, too, and when they saw us lagging back they started teasing us in Spanish and trying to stir us up to a tomato fight.

"*Ay,*" one of them said to Mason, "*chico, mira.*"

He pointed at Benjy who was bent over in a nearby row slowly picking away.

"What?" Mason asked. *"Qúe?"* The *bracero* made a throwing motion. "Oh, *yo entiendo.* I get it."

Picking up a bad tomato, Mason sighted in on Benjy's rear end and let fly. It made a big splat on his jeans.

"Hey," Benjy yelled. He turned around all mad until he saw who did it. "You'll pay for that, buster." He fired a tomato back. It whistled by Mason's head.

The *braceros* watched us and laughed, so I threw a tomato and hit Mason in the side. Pretty soon it was a madhouse out there. It only lasted a couple of minutes but even some of the *braceros* got into it for a second. When it was over there were smashed tomatoes all over the place and us *gringos* looked pretty messy.

The day finally ended at three-thirty and me and Jim and Benjy went up and got our crates tallied and our pay. Benjy broke even, Mason had to take the hourly wage to get his dollar an hour, and I made just over the minimum.

"Who made the most out here?" I asked the field boss. We all wanted to know.

"One of the new guys," he answered. "A kid from down below Mexicali. Alvarado or Alvarez, somethin' like that."

"How much?"

"He made thirty-two fifty."

"Better'n three times minimum pay."

"Jesus, these guys kick ass," Benjy said. We climbed on board the truck for the trip back to town.

"Don't I know it," I said.

"I'm whipped," Mason said.

We slumped in the narrow wooden seats on the inside of the truck. Smoke belching from its exhaust, the old, rattletrap vehicle jerked forward and banged along the dusty road back to town.

Next day we thinned cotton with short-handled hoes again. A week from that Friday we all quit the fields. It was the same every year. Who would want to do that kind of stuff for a living, unless you had to? We were lucky. We didn't have to do it. So we didn't.

Just Waiting On You, Gordon

"Last Flight" by Larry Fultz—Used by Permission of Author

The first time PFC Billy Travis laid eyes on Gordon Todwiler, the stocky Corporal was burning human feces at Base Camp Rutledge. The makeshift latrines used at Camp Rutledge were actually 55-gallon barrels cut in half and the army's solution to the waste removal problem was to burn it where it was.

Gordon was a big old boy, raw-boned, sandy-haired, soft spoken, and steady. Billy held his nose with his left hand and tapped his jungle hat with the forefinger of his right hand in greeting. With as much irony removed from his voice as possible he asked the younger man how he liked the army so far. Gordon looked up from pouring what looked to be about 30 gallons of diesel fuel on the feces and smiled.

"Shoot, this ain't bad," he said. "I had worse jobs back home."

"Where's home?"

"Arkansas."

"No kiddin'? Me, too."

"Whereabouts?"

Gordon stepped back from the fuel-soaked feces and pulled out a Zippo lighter. He then held up a light piece of stained white cloth. Billy moved back a few feet.

"Greenfield," he told Gordon, eyeing the zippo and the cloth. "Pretty close to Fayetteville."

"Well, I'll be danged," Gordon said, "I'm from right there my ownself. I'm from Elm Springs."

"Shoot, we're practically neighbors. Howdy neighbor."

"Howdy your ownself."

He reached out a hand, which Billy did not move forward to shake. Gordon looked down at his hand and laughed.

"Sorry, none too appealing I suppose."

"None, too. Name's Billy Travis. What's your'n?"

"Gordon Todwiler. Pleased to me you."

"Likewise."

"You might oughten to step back just a bit more." Billy watched Gordon light the soiled rag.

"Yes, sir, I believe I'll slide over here a ways." Gordon smiled. "Here goes."

Gordon tossed the flaming rag on the fuel-sated feces. There was a resounding boom and an explosion of flame that shot up four feet or more. Both men laughed and Billy headed for safer pastures—downwind. Definitely downwind.

"See ya, Billy."

"See ya."

Billy hustled out of the area. The odor of the burning waste still caught up with him and he put a hand over his nose and mouth as he jogged through camp away from Gordon's pyrotechnics.

•   •   •

Billy arrived in Viet Nam on 9 July 1966. He was on his second hitch in the army, having gotten out for a restless year and then re-upped in early '66. Billy did his AIT, specializing in helicopter gunship weapons repair, on the second hitch at the Aberdeen Proving Grounds in Maryland. Gordon, Billy soon learned, was a first-termer, a draftee, and had done his basic training at Fort

Leonard Wood in Missouri and then AIT at Fort Polk's famous "Tigerland" down in Louisiana. Gordon was first assigned to an armored division in Germany, but spent only a few months there before being shipped to the war zone.

The two new friends arrived at Base Camp Rutledge in the Central Highlands of Viet Nam within a week of each other. In another week they met each other over the fine odor of human waste. They had Arkansas in common. Billy's home, Greenfield, was a country community about 10 miles northeast of Fayetteville, and Elm Springs, Gordon's birthplace, was a similar farming community maybe 15 miles northwest of Fayetteville.

They became fast friends right away. While they waited for their new unit to come back in out of the field, Billy learned that Gordon had been trained in armor, on tanks, and that just bad timing and luck had gotten him reassigned from Germany to an Air Cav division in Nam. They were members of the 1st Cavalry Air Mobile, until recently the 1st Cavalry Division and later to be the 1st Air Cavalry, Troop B of the 1st Battalion of the 9th Cavalry. The 1st of the 9th in Army lingo.

For two weeks, while their unit provided troop transport support for a U.S.-South Vietnamese operation in the Highlands bush, Gordon and Billy and about a half-dozen other new troops, or FNGs as they were called, went through additional training by an older sergeant and a couple of specialists left behind at base camp. The newcomers also got sent out on night patrols near the camp and practiced rappelling from an old Huey that threatened to go down of its own accord on every flight.

The rest of the time they did what soldiers have done for years—they policed the area of cigarette butts and trash, stacked and restacked the same supplies under hot metal-roofed storage buildings, and painted anything that didn't move in the camp and that wasn't already painted army olive drab.

When their unit returned from the field, tired, dirty, and ill-tempered, but with only a couple of lightly-wounded casualties, Billy and the others began the process of blending in. Billy's job specialty, his MOS, was weapons repair and he started his new job right away. He worked on the UH-1B "Huey" choppers, fixing rockets, grenade launchers, and modified M-60 machine guns mounted on each side of the helicopters and controlled by electric and hydraulic cabling.

When he wasn't working on weapons, Billy volunteered for door gunner duty on those same Hueys. The jungle beyond Base Camp Rutledge saw plenty of action and due to losses and exhaustion, the units always needed somebody to man the M-60s on chopper flights.

Billy also volunteered for infantry duty with Gordon's company—or more accurately, he agreed to go out with Gordon's squad when they were undermanned. Early on at Camp Rutledge, Billy began to have doubts, maybe just questions at first, about the purpose of the war.

Throughout his previous hitch, Billy clung to the values that had made him enlist. He believed in being honest, in doing your duty, in keeping faith in God, in standing up for your country— right or wrong. Most of the men and boys he met in the army didn't hold those same values and much of the time Billy felt he was under siege, as if his beliefs were somehow old-fashioned, out of date, irrelevant.

Reports from back home almost always had new stories of anti-war protests and a questioning of the mission in this far away place. Billy didn't pay much heed to the protestors. But they mildly annoyed him because they didn't really know what it was like for the average grunt fighting this increasingly odd little war. Still, what he saw happening in the villages and countryside in which he and his unit fought troubled him.

Whenever his unit contacted villages in the company of regular South Vietnamese, ARVN, forces, Billy saw that the locals despised and feared their own army. The villagers, in their poverty and rags, were alienated from the very army whose putative mission was their protection and support.

That the United States supported such a government and army seemed to be out of sync with American ideals. An attitude became current with Billy and his fellow GIs that defending yourself, surviving the war, was the only goal. Stay alive, go home. Forget about it. Handle what was right in front of you and let the rest go. Their goal was a simple on. Live through the twelve month hitch and get back to the world—in one piece.

Billy, being a country boy, was good at surviving. He had skills. He was a keen marksman and because he grew up in the Ozarks hills he was really good in the bush. On one of the first missions with Gordon's unit in the field, Billy discovered a cache of radio equipment. The VC stashed it in a cave-like depression just off the trail the unit was moving along on a search and engage mission far from their base camp in the jungle near the Cambodian border.

"What's that you got there, Travis?" Sgt. Walker, Gordon's squad leader, walked back down the trail to where Billy and Gordon were in the bush investigating the unexpected find.

"Billy found a bunch of radios, Sarge," Gordon explained.

Sgt. Walker looked over the equipment. It was Army olive drab, O.D., but it had no markings of any kind.

"Sarge," another grunt from Gordon's squad called from the nearby bush. "Lookie here."

Circling the new find cautiously, the squad poked and pulled at the jungle carefully, revealing several large pieces of blue and white metal.

"What do you reckon all this stuff is?" Gordon wondered. He looked over at Billy, who twisted an eye up in response.

"This was some sort of small aircraft," Sgt. Walker turned over what looked like a chunk of wing with his jungle boots. "What do you think, Travis?"

"Well, Sarge," Billy rubbed his chin with his right thumb and forefinger. "I believe I've seen those markings before."

"Exactly," the sergeant said. "Me, too."

"So what is it?" one of the other men asked.

"If me and Travis are on the same page," Sgt. Walker said, "this looks like a company crash."

"Company?" Gordon asked.

"The CIA," Sgt. Walker explained.

"Wow," Gordon exclaimed with a wide-eyed grin at Billy. "Son of a gun."

"Is that what you were thinking, Travis?" the sergeant asked Billy.

"Yep, I reckon it was," Billy said laconically, pointing at the metal. "It's that blue and white painting."

"Right," Sgt. Walker agreed. "Air America. The spooks have been here, boys."

"Whew," Gordon shook his head, "ain't that somethin'."

"Well, we took enough time here." Sgt. Walker told the unit. "Fall in. Let's hump it. Travis, you take point and get us the hell out of here."

"All right, sergeant," Billy drawled.

The troop moved back out of the bush and onto the barely trod path they followed.

"Don't worry, Billy," Gordon patted Billy on the shoulder. "I'm right here behind you."

"I wasn't worried," Billy said without looking back. "I knowed you was there."

• • •

On 27 August 1966, Billy and his chopper crew were sent to the Special Forces camp Plei Me near the Cambodian border. Operation Frontier it was called, which the troops immediately renamed Operation Front and Rear because the enemy was on both sides of them in Cambodia and Viet Nam.

The next day, Billy's crew landed at a remote camp late in the afternoon. They brought in supplies for the boonie rats stuck there in the forgotten jungle. After he unloaded the chopper, Billy stayed back to work on a fault in the hydraulic system. He became so engrossed in his work he didn't notice the time, and suddenly it was getting dark. He had way missed the five p.m. curfew to be back in camp.

"Crap," he admonished himself as he cleaned up his wrenches and mopped down the chopper. "What the heck am I going to do?"

Dusk settled in deeply then and he knew he couldn't get back to the firebase. Some nervous Nelly would waste him for sure if he came rustling out of the bush in the dark. If he called out they would probably just fire on the sound and Charlie might be somewhere nearby, anyway. With no alternative, Billy holed up inside the chopper and hoped it didn't take a direct mortar round or missile from some VC or NVA lurking in the black jungle.

All went well until shortly before midnight. Billy heard sounds outside the Huey. He had an M-16 and a .45 pistol but he knew his best bet, if it turned out to be a single sapper, was to try to take him out with a knife. From his first days in Nam, Billy carried a boot knife—a nasty, serrated five-inch blade that he kept sharpened to a hair-slicing fine edge. It was a killing knife and he intended to use if he had to.

Hiding in the blackness by the grunt seats near the side sliding doors, Billy breathed softly, quietly, waiting for the VC to make a move. Seconds, minutes passed by as slowly as geological eras. Then the sapper reached into the chopper with one arm, the other loaded with his satchel charge. Billy grabbed the VC's free arm and pulled it hard. Before the man could react, the cold, sharp edge of Billy's rough-bladed knife split the skin of the enemy's neck and carved deeper, through muscle, sinew, vein, artery. With a grunting cough the VC fell backwards away from the Huey to the jungle floor, blood pouring from his lifeless body.

Next day, when Billy made it back to camp, he said nothing about the sapper. But his crew, when they saw the bloody scene by the chopper, understood exactly what had happened. Word spread quickly and both Billy's crew and the boonie rats of Plei Me looked at the young weapons repairman in an entirely different way.

During late summer and early fall—if it could be called that in the jungle—Billy began a project so unexpected he sometimes felt he was being directed by an unseen hand. He started writing a poem. At first he only wrote snatches of it in his mind, then, if he could find a pen handy, he wrote a line or two on a scrap piece of paper or the back of a napkin. Finally, he bought himself a small notebook and ballpoint pen at the base camp's makeshift PX and started working on the poem whenever he had the free time.

"What you doing there, Billy?" Gordon asked one afternoon when they both happened to be in camp with some free time.

"Writing."

"Writing? Writing to your mama?"

"Just writing."

Gordon scratched his head. "What would you write?"

"I don't know what it is. Maybe a poem?"

"A poem?" Gordon whistled. "Shoot, I ain't never known anybody wrote a poem before."

"My aunts write poems," Billy said. "Don't recall if my mama ever did, though."

"My mama mostly tanned my hide."

"Mine, too."

"Can I read what you wrote?"

"Aah..."

"If you don't want me to."

"No, no," Billy assured his friend, "it's okay."

He handed the notepad to Gordon, who looked it over with a puzzled expression.

"Maybe it would work better if you read it out loud. I ain't much of a reader."

"You sure?"

"Shoot," Gordon shrugged. "I don't know nothin' at all about it. Go on."

"All right," Billy said. "Here goes. It ain't done yet, but I got some verses done. I'm calling it 'Last Flight.'"

Gordon nodded. Billy read.

There's smoke ahead as we make a turn,
Our tracers streaking by,
If Charlie's out there in the bush
You know he can bend over
And kiss his ass goodbye.

The rockets roar
The 50s clatter
The blades are poppin' hard
We see Charlie running now
Across the paddies below
But it seems he's getting' tired.

"This is gonna be easy,"
The pilot says
"Like a pond full of sittin' ducks."
But then the crew chief yells
"Get outta here,
We just run outta luck."

"Is that it?" Gordon asked. "Don't you got some more of it?"
"I do have more."
"Go on, then. Read it"
"I'll read it."

Too late we find
As we make our pass
A 50's waitin' there.
The chopper's hit
The pilot slumps
He now no longer cares.

The co-pilot reaches over
As quick as he can
To take hold of the stick
Then he's hit, too,
We're going down,
Man, I'm feelin' sick.

We hit ground hard
The bird's on fire
I'm thrown clear of the mess
I look around
But I'm the only one
That made it out I guess.

Then I hear a sound
A sound so sweet,
The chase bird is in sight.
If they can only
Spot me now
I might live through this fight.

"That's all I have so far."

"Wow," Gordon exclaimed. "That's just like it is out there, ain't it?"

"You think?"

"Sure it is. That's real good, Billy. You gonna do more of it?"

"I reckon. I don't rightfully know right now. But it ain't finished. That's for sure."

"Well that was pretty darn good. Course I ain't got much know how when it comes to poems and such."

"Me neither," Billy said.

• • •

Over the next few weeks Billy didn't see much of Gordon. Gordon's outfit kept being shipped off to different places than Billy's crews, but they ran into each other from time to time. On 12 October, Billy's ship and crew flew some grunts into a cold LZ near Cambodia and were loading back up with several wounded when all hell suddenly broke loose on the hastily put together camp.

Rocket and mortar fire rained down for the better part of an afternoon and into the evening. Billy and his crew hit the dugout trenches in the camp and stayed hunkered down just as low as they possibly could until the barrage slowly waned, then stopped sometime near midnight.

The following day was the most explosive Billy had ever seen. F-4s roared overhead all day, saturating the bush beyond camp with 500 pound bombs and an occasional napalm drop. Sometimes the bombing and burning would get so close that the ground shook and the oxygen seemed to be sucked from the very atmosphere as the dug in troops waited out the siege. By late afternoon, Billy and the others could hear small arms fire in the bush and the familiar thump-thump-thumping of support and fire Hueys, but Billy's own crew stayed put.

Next morning dawned bright and blue and steamy hot. Except for distant smoke and debris around the camp from the shelling, it could have been another day in a tropical paradise. Before his chopper headed out, an inspired Billy jotted down four more verses to his poem.

> They make a pass
> Charlie's 50s gone
> And down they bank for me.
> I'm standing up
> A wavin' hard
> But Charlie too can see.
>
> Still they lit down, and
> I climb on board.
> "Come on we're outta here."
> Then I get a funny feelin'
> I didn't have before—I ain't sure but
> I think it might be fear.
>
> More birds arrive
> The fight is over
> And finally we are gone

It was my last flight
I'm glad of that
And soon I'm going home.

But what about
The ones still there
The guys I left behind?
I'll never see
Their faces again
But they're always on my mind.

•   •   •

In November, the powers that be decided to really get after Charlie. Some armchair general dubbed the new offensive Operation Push Back, and that's what the units of the 1st Air Cav did, push back on the VC. Billy and Gordon's outfit led the mission and the two friends were almost always in the field—Gordon with the infantry, Billy working door gunner/ weapons repair on the Huey crews that ferried Gordon's outfit all over the bush.

On the bright, clear morning of 12 November, Gordon's unit was dropped off about twenty clicks from Camp Rutledge in a somewhat warm LZ. Gordon was on Billy's Huey and the buddies exchanged informal hand salutes as the grunts dropped out of the chopper and into the tall grass of the LZ.

"Kick some butt, Gordon," Billy told his friend as Gordon piled out of the machine.

"We'll try, Billy," Gordon smiled his patented country boy ear-to-ear grin. The sound of rifle fire cut short the goodbye and while Gordon's squad hustled for cover, Billy's chopper quickly lifted off and headed into the deep blue Viet Nam sky.

Over the next couple of hours, Billy's crew ferried several groups of grunts where they were needed in the bush. Around mid-day, the bird let off another batch of soldiers and then under some duress from nearby entrenched VC hurriedly sped away with a couple of lightly-wounded GIs in tow.

They were about forty minutes out from the drop, still flying low and fast as they had all day, when they came under heavy enemy fire. Rounds whizzed by the chopper, occasionally hitting against it with the metallic slaps and pops that no crewmember ever liked to hear. Billy returned fire at any puff of smoke or flash of fire that he could see. Suddenly, several rounds hit the machine flush on and the chopper lurched, jerked—almost like a bucking horse—settled for a moment and then, unmistakably, began to lose altitude.

Billy fired at the tree line below but heard through his helmet mike the concern in the pilot's and co-pilot's voices. He could hear Baker, manning the gun on the opposite door, and saw the fear in the eyes of the two wounded GIs.

The Huey, its hydraulic system badly damaged, spun dizzily as it dropped. The pilot called out a Mayday, sent their coordinates, talked to nearby units on the ground. Just before the chopper crashed, Billy heard a familiar voice from the bush—the radioman from Gordon's outfit—as well as that of the co-pilot telling the crew what it already knew.

"We're going in," he cried over the intercom radio. "Mayday. Mayday. We're going in."

Then, with an impact none of the men could have prepared for, the Huey ripped through the jungle canopy, smashed through the trees, and slammed into the ground. Tree limbs and bushes jabbed through the open doors and broke out the windows. The crew smelled leaking fuel and heard the snapping of broken electrical short circuits—miraculously nothing caught on fire.

The chopper, finally not moving, was tilted slightly to starboard, not quite level with the ground, the front down and touching the jungle floor. Billy unstrapped himself, grabbed one of the injured GI's M-16 and hustled out the door. He pushed through some thick shrubs to get to a small clearing near the wreckage. The pilots, Baker, and the stunned GIs found their way out as well.

"Is everyone okay?" the co-pilot asked. Except for some bumps and bruises everyone was.

"We gotta be on our toes, guys." the pilot told the group. "Charlie's all over the damned place. The radio is stone dead, so we're on our own until some of our guys come get us. Until then, we better set up a perimeter around the bird. Baker and Travis, help get those wounded men back inside. They'll be better off there for the time being."

"Yes, sir," Billy said. He and Baker helped the hurt GIs back on board the helicopter.

There was a long stretch then, maybe fifteen to twenty minutes—it seemed like hours to the men—where the group heard nothing but the sounds of distant combat. They watched the jungle around them, listened for nearby noise.

"Travis," the pilot broke a long nervous silence, climb up to the bird and see if you can spot anything out in the bush.

"Yes, sir."

With the alacrity of youth, Billy scrambled onto the Huey and stood up slowly. He surveyed the area but the foliage was so dense there was little to see. He signaled to the others that there was nothing out there. He heard a chopper somewhere to the north of their position, but could never spot it. After several minutes, the pilot motioned for Billy to come down.

Another slow-moving twenty to thirty minutes passed. Billy felt the tension among his comrades but for some reason he felt calm, alert but tranquil. That was when he heard the first sound. The co-pilot heard the sound, too, but Billy held up a finger to keep him from speaking.

Slowly, Billy moved away from the Huey, walking towards the brush to the right of their position. Billy lifted the M-16 and aimed it toward the sound, watching the bush closely. The tall grass moved, pushed forward, began to spread out. Billy held the rifle ready, his aim just to the left of the disturbance. Then the grass opened out, revealing a face. A round, familiar face. Billy paused. The face was smiling broadly.

"What'cha doing, Billy?" Gordon's irrepressibly friendly voice drawled.

Billy heard the sigh of relief from the rest of the men behind him. He lowered his M-16 and smiled back at his friend.

"Just waitin' on you, Gordon," he said as calmly as if they were all in line at the chow hall and a buddy had arrived a couple of minutes late. "Just waitin' on you."

• • •

After the crash, Billy's crew got some downtime back at Camp Rutledge. Through the holidays and into the new year things were relatively quiet, but then in early February action picked up again. It was back to the same old routine—in and out of hot LZs, picking up and dropping off GIs in the bush.

On 9 February, they dropped Gordon and his squad in the general vicinity of the November crash. Billy gave Gordon a thumbs-up from the door of the chopper and Gordon smiled that country boy smile again. Flying back to base camp Billy laughed thinking of his easygoing friend. Three days later he learned Gordon died in a firefight with a large NVA unit that crossed over into Viet Nam from Cambodia.

Billy never spoke of Gordon's death, and he never cried about it. But from that day on he stopped volunteering for door gunner duty. He did his job as weapons repairman but whatever drive he once had was gone. He was a soldier and a good one, but there was no feeling left.

When he rotated to the states after his full tour, Billy passed through the huge military hub at Tachikawa Air Base near Tokyo. Sitting on the edge of his cot in the transient airman's quarters, he visualized himself at some point in his own future, and wrote the last two verses of his poem.

> *Now the years have come,*
> *The years have gone*
> *And I'm gettin' old.*
> *The memories of the years at war*
> *Will fade soon I am told.*
>
> *But though I live*
> *A hundred years*
> *Their faces I'll still see.*
> *And as I get*
> *Both old and gray*
> *They'll always be young to me.*

After a two day wait, Billy caught a civilian flight to San Francisco. Less than twenty-four hours later he was back in the Arkansas Ozarks, disoriented, unsure of himself, but moving on with his life. He considered going over to Gordon's little town and paying his respects at the graveyard and with his friend's family—but he could never muster the energy for it.

He soon found that no one back home wanted to know anything about Nam, especially friendships made, friends lost.

So Billy left everything inside where he'd put it anyway. It was something you had to live with on your own. You really didn't have much of a choice. There was nothing for it.

Morena

"Will you be going to the mainland soon, Charles?" Dr. Rakes asked above the general noise of the University of Boca Tierra English Department End-of-Semester party. "Now that you are graduating?"

"No, Dr. Rakes," Charles said, setting down an empty bottle of beer. "I've been offered a contract at Inter-Caribbean."

"Oh, how wonderful. I didn't know."

"Just found out this morning myself."

"Inter-Caribbean is a wonderful school," Dr. Rakes allowed. "Although we think we're a step better here at UBT."

"Yes, ma'am," Charles nodded.

"Well, Maggie," Dr. Rakes addressed the pretty, brown-skinned girl standing beside Charles, "I should think you'll be pleased. I dare say you weren't looking forward to him leaving our little island."

"No, I wasn't, Dr. Rakes," Maggie replied.

"Have you a job as well, my dear?"

"Oh, no, mum," Maggie said in a lilting Barbadian accent. "I still have the summer to go. I won't graduate until August. After that I'm really not sure."

"I see. Well, best wishes to both of you. I see Dr. Bourne and I must talk to him about who will be acting department head while he's gone this summer. I hope you will be happy. I have to run. Goodbye."

"Isn't she sweet," Maggie said, when Rakes was out of earshot.

"She's getting up there a little though," Charles winked.

"Charles," Maggie scolded.

"Well, she is."

"You needn't say so. Now, get me another drink. It's your punishment."

"My what?"

"Your punishment."

Charles laughed, but went to get the drinks, mixing Maggie a gin and tonic and getting himself another beer. When he got back, she seemed, in just that little time, distant and vaguely angry.

"What's wrong?" He handed Maggie her drink and popped the top off his beer. "I know that look. Something's up. Was it what Dr. Rakes said? The end of summer is a long way away yet, you know."

Maggie took a moment to answer. She stared through Charles as if he were someone she didn't know. He hated that look.

"Forget it, let's just enjoy the party."

"We'll have to face this sooner or later, Charles."

"Not now, Maggie, we're supposed to be celebrating the end of the semester. This isn't the place or time to decide our future."

"Your future, you mean."

"Come on. That's not fair."

Opportunely, Charles noticed Dan McGuire across the room and waved to him. Dan raised a bottle of beer in salute. Charles held his up in return. He missed what Maggie said.

"What?" he said. "There's Dan by the table. See him?"

"Yes, I see him. I said it is fair. You're not listening."

"This is supposed to be a party. Let's go visit Dan awhile. You say he always cheers you up. Come on."

Charles tugged on Maggie's arm. She scowled but let him pull her towards Dan and the refreshment table.

"You're not always going to get away with this, Charles."

"I know, baby, I know. Let's just have fun today, Okay? Forget it, please?"

"Forget what?" Dan asked as the couple neared him.

"Oh, nothing, pal," Charles said. "Nothing. We were just talking. Right, Maggie?"

Maggie turned away from Charles and smiled at Dan. He smiled back.

• • •

Maggie toweled dry in the large shower stall at Charles' apartment in the heart of its bustling capitol, San Sebastian. She pulled the shower curtain back and Charles, wearing only his shorts, watched her movements in the mirror over the little sink.

"Morena," he said softly.

"What?" Maggie said, looking up.

"Beautiful brown woman. Morena."

Maggie smiled. Charles turned away from the mirror to look directly at her. He felt a sharp pang that was somewhere between pleasure and pain. She was so pretty. So lean yet finely shaped, with a casual, understated sexuality. Charles thought of how soon summer would end and of the personal choices each of them would have to make. He wanted things to stay the way they were now. He wanted to remember this particular image of her forever.

Moving forward, he took the towel from Maggie's hand. She stepped out of the shower onto the rug. He ran his hand along her bare shoulder.

"You're after something," she grinned.

He moved closer to her, pressing against her.

"Charles," Maggie said quietly.

He held her closer, pushed her long, thick hair back, kissed her on the shoulders, neck, and cheeks. She lowered her head and turned towards him. He felt the warm solidness of her mouth against his.

"Come on," he said.

"Charles," she said, catching her breath.

"Please," he said. "Please."

•   •   •

When Maggie was thirteen, something unusual happened to her. It wasn't a particular incident, no special life-changing trauma, nor was it the first onset of her progress towards becoming a woman. No, she couldn't link it to any specific event, date, time, or place, but during her thirteenth year a feeling grew within her, spread from a small place deep inside to eventually inform the very essence of who she was and who she was to be.

She couldn't put a name to this feeling, this sense, but she came to know its symptoms all too well. It manifested itself in an intellectual restlessness, an intermittent physical ennui, a feeling of dissatisfaction that tainted her daily life with an uncomfortable and unexplained feeling of unhappiness. She assumed it was what every teenager experienced, and she was right. Yet as time passed and the feeling didn't, she began to think that this gnawing, depressing sense of unfulfillment was more than just a natural phase that would pass. That it was who she was, who she had become, that it was permanent.

Simply growing up helped Maggie, to an extent. The sharpness of the pain diminished, even disappeared for days, weeks at a time. She would feel normal for a while, find herself involved with new friends, with community activities, even with another in a limited series of young beaus who were attracted to her endearing shyness and undeniable good looks.

But the boyfriends were like everything else in Maggie's life—temporary and unsatisfying. The guys were too shallow, or too physically aggressive, or too unwilling to go that extra step towards serious involvement. As a result they became like everything else seemed to be in Maggie's life—unable to live up to its billing.

When she first met Charles in college, it seemed that he might be what she had been looking for. That something she had never been able to define but was sure she would know if it ever presented itself to her. And for the better part of the next year Charles did fit the bill. He was fun, kind, solicitous of her needs, anxious to make her happy. They had a nice time together. For quite a while.

But lately, as he neared graduation and she summer school, the old dissatisfaction, the restlessness, the undefined need had begun to reassert itself. She found she was short with Charles, saw faults in him she had not noticed before, felt compelled, against her will it seemed, to withdraw from him, to go back into herself. By the end of the spring semester she felt their relationship had turned a corner she wasn't sure they could come back around.

• • •

"Smile." Charles reached across the table in the small restaurant and took one of Maggie's long, slender hands in his. She smiled but there was no joy in her deep brown eyes. "You have the saddest eyes I've ever seen. What's wrong?"

"I'm not sad, I'm preoccupied."

"Well, preoccupied, then," Charles laughed.

"It's not funny."

"No, I guess not. I just—"

"Not now." Maggie cut him off as their waitress arrived with menus.

She chose a salad, Charles a large bean burrito. When the waitress left, the couple sat quietly for several moments, each looking around the uncrowded restaurant. Finally, Charles broke the silence.

"You just gonna clam up on me?"

"Clam up on you?" she laughed.

"She smiles, she laughs. What's next, fun? That would be a rare treat." Maggie's mood clouded. "Oh, crap," Charles backtracked, "I didn't mean anything." Maggie shook her head. "God, Maggie, we've got to get past this."

"We will get past this."

"Yeah, but past it together?"

Maggie leaned back in her chair and sighed. Charles didn't look at her. When the food came, they ate slowly, silently, without pleasure.

•   •   •

Charles handed a glass of cola across the bed to Maggie. They were comfortably propped up on large pillows, feeling a warm wind stir through the room from the open Miami windows and watching a Spanish-language rerun of *Bonanza*.

"This part here is great," Charles explained, "Little Joe and Candy are going to fight over that woman. I've seen this episode about ten times."

"How foolish," Maggie commented.

"Well, TV is not too hot down here."

"No, no, I mean to fight for the woman. It makes her become some piece of property that goes to the victor."

"Well, that's the way it was," Charles said, trying to steer clear of an overworked topic between them.

"Is," Maggie corrected. "She has nothing to say in the matter. They decide her fate."

"Maggie, it's just a show. TV. And an old show at that."

"For women it's still the same."

"Pass me the coke, will you."

Maggie handed him the glass. He took a drink and set the glass on the bed stand.

"Look at those imbeciles," Maggie watched the TV characters engage in a rollicking fistfight while a demure young woman stood to the side, helplessly waving her arms. "You're just like those two. You never consider giving us a choice. Not even today. Do you?"

"Maggie, it's just a show for Christ's sake. That's not the way it is nowadays, and you know it. Especially not with me and you."

"Humph."

"Okay, come on. We've been over the real problem before. This sideways stuff is crazy."

Charles looked at Maggie's pretty face and saw the concern there. She was caught between destinies—his and hers. He knew that. It didn't make things any easier.

"Morena, I love you. I don't want to use you, or just take from you. I want to share my life with you—our life."

She regarded him as if she were trying to read into his eyes or find something about herself in the reflection she found there.

"I know you do, Charles." She sighed. "And I love you too. It's just that..."

• • •

They met late outside the UBT administration building when the heat of the day was nearly gone, when the tranquil light of the coming sunset bathed the campus in a soft yellow glow. Walking slowly across the lush old campus, they spoke quietly and calmly.

"You won't come with me to Inter-Caribbean?" Charles asked.

"I'm going to spend some time at home."

"Right after you graduate?"

"Yes."

"Couldn't you come up before you go?"

"I want to go to home and visit my family before I make up my mind about grad school."

"You'll have to decide pretty fast if you're going to get in anywhere by fall."

"Yes I know. I'm perfectly aware of that."

Charles elected not to react to what he perceived as Maggie's latest bait. Over the last months she had matched her moments of indifference with episodes of combativeness. Despite recent difficulties she was an affectionate, bright young woman. A real catch for the right guy. But lately Charles felt perhaps he was not that guy—maybe no guy could be.

Charles, attentive and quiet now, was almost certainly not the answer for Maggie. As they walked on, she surprised him by casually taking his hand. He looked at her in the soft light.

"Want to pick up something and go back to your place?"

"Sure," she said. "I guess so. Okay."

• • •

Charles's day-long visit to Inter-Caribbean went well. The graduate advisor, a Dr. Vega, was amiable and helpful, the other teaching assistants engaging and friendly. The morning sped by as Charles and his fellow incoming TAs were greeted with a series of brief introductory mini-lectures on their duties and responsibilities at I-C. Then they were hustled about campus to get familiar with the student union, the library, and other facilities on the rapidly growing, out-island college.

For lunch, Charles joined a handful of his new acquaintances—including a couple of girls who seemed to find him interesting—for sandwiches at a little café popular with the students and younger faculty. The afternoon sessions were given over to short teaching forums and several pep talks delivered by the department head, a couple of professors and three or four veteran TAs.

At day's end, reluctant to head straight back home, Charles hooked up with one of the friendlier girls, a pretty native named Eloisa. They found a bar not far from campus, another student and younger faculty hangout, and had several drinks together. During the two hours or so they spent together at the bar, Charles did not mention Maggie or his life with her.

Only a little over sixty miles from San Sebastian, yet nearly an hour and a half drive on the island's narrow little roads, the seemingly distant world of Inter-Caribbean made Charles feel like he was an entirely different person. A person unfettered and uninvolved, free to live as he pleased. When Eloisa had to leave about six, Charles said goodbye and, with her promise to get together when they started the fall semester echoing in his thoughts, drove back home in good spirits. He got back about seven-thirty and tried to call Maggie but she had gone out.

Just as well, he thought. He was tired from the trip and wanted to hang onto his good mood. He hated to admit it but that might not have been possible if Maggie had been home. Settling in, Charles filled a big glass with coke and lots of ice and began to organize his belongings for the move to Inter-Caribbean.

• • •

An Eastern 1011 lumbered down the runway, straining to reach takeoff speed, then slowly, with surprising grace, lifted off into the bright Caribbean sky. Charles watched the jet as it climbed over the blue-green bay beyond the airport and began to turn in a slow curve to the left, away from the island, away from Boca Tierra. When he brought his attention back to the inside of the airport, Maggie was beside him.

"Are you ready?" he asked.

"Yes."

They stood side by side in the waiting room near Gate 12B, not touching.

"Won't you reconsider?"

"No, Charles, not now."

"I'm going to fly over as soon as possible."

"As you wish."

"Maggie."

"There's nothing more to say."

"I still love you," Charles said, not sure if he really did.

Maggie looked away. The passengers nearby moved towards the gate. Maggie took out the flight ticket from her carry-on bag.

"I do," Charles insisted. Maggie's flight was announced.

"Goodbye, Charles," she said as they approached the outer door. Charles could go no further.

"Maggie," he said plaintively.

Maggie leaned against him and they embraced. He kissed her cheek. She pulled away, eyes filling with tears.

"Maggie," he whispered.

"Goodbye, Charles." She squared her shoulders proudly, then hurried away.

Charles stood there alone, watching the door through

which she had gone. After a few moments, he went to the windows at the back of the room and looked out. It took a few seconds for his eyes to adjust to the outdoor sunlight, but then he saw her, waiting in line near the steps leading up into the plane. Her back was to him and he couldn't tell what she was feeling as she prepared to leave his life. He wasn't sure what he was feeling either, but he had to admit he made no physical effort to stop her from going.

For several minutes boarding was delayed, then he saw her climb up the stairs and, without looking back, enter the plane. He stared out at the runway, shielding his eyes from the glare off the window. In a few moments, the plane taxied to the end of the runway. After a brief pause, it began its takeoff. He watched it build up speed, lift off, and in a slow arc, turn and climb, up—away. Away from Boca Tierra. Away from him.

Charles looked past the San Sebastian skyline to the distant mountains of the El Grande range. Framed in the deep blue Caribbean sky, El Grande itself rose up green and majestic from the Boca Tierran countryside, clean and natural beyond the exhaust-smoke filled skies of the city. He watched Maggie's plane until it became a white speck and faded into the far sky. Taking a deep breath, Charles turned and walked out of the terminal building and crossed the parking lot to his car. He had a long drive ahead of him.

Papi

This time they found Papi four blocks from home in the Plaza del Caribe Mall. He was wandering around—lost, feverish, asking for help to get to Miami. Alfonso raced out to get him about six-thirty and the security guard, who was locking up the mall, had been rather rude.

"You'd better control this old man." The guard carefully checked Alfonso's identification. Papi sat in a chair nearby, apparently not comprehending.

"Certainly," Alfonso said, annoyed at the guard's tone.

"He's a public menace."

"He's an old man. Old and sick. That's as plain as the nose on your face."

"Well, get him out of here. Next time I call the police."

"There won't be a next time." Alfonso helped Papi up, putting his right arm around the old man's bony shoulder as support. "Come on, father. Let's go." He glared back at the guard who snorted in disgust.

"Gusanos," the guard muttered as Alfonso led his father away. Alfonso stopped. He turned back toward the guard.

"What's that?"

"Nothing, just move along. Take the old man out of here."

Enraged, Alfonso mumbled a curse, but led Papi away.

At home, he put his father to bed and sat by him most of the night while the old man tossed and turned in feverish pain. Early next morning, Alfonso's wife, Eloisa, came into the guest bedroom and cleaned her father-in-law's sweat-covered face with a cool cloth. Alfonso pressed her free hand and smiled weakly. Eloisa kissed him on the forehead and patted his tired shoulders.

"He was trying to go to Miami," Alfonso said. "Como siempre. Like he always does."

"I know," Eloisa said, wiping the old man's brow. He stirred slightly and his eyes opened briefly. "Alfonso," Eloisa said.

"I see," Alfonso said. They looked down at the old man. He looked very old and very tired.

"Papi," Eloisa said, "can you hear me? Are you comfortable?"

"Miami," Papi managed to get out. When he pronounced the word it sounded like *mee-ahm-ee*. *"Miami,"* he said again hoarsely. *"Un kiosk . . . hermanos."*

"He's delirious," Alfonso said. "It's the fever."

Eloisa nodded and went to soak the face cloth with cold water. When she returned, the old man was still very hot and incoherent. "Oh, Papi," she said, wiping his face gently. "Poor Papi."

Alfonso got up and walked to the jalousied bedroom window. He looked outside at the neighboring yards with their green lawns, rubber plants, and avocado trees. Miami windows, he thought with irony, Miami. Poor Papi.

"Miami," the old man blurted out again. Alfonso jumped. It was like his father read his mind.

"Papi," Eloisa pleaded soothingly. "Please. You have to stop thinking of Miami. You must rest. You're sick."

"He always loved Miami," Alfonso said reflectively.

"Yes, though I don't know why."

"It was because there were so many of his generation there. They wanted to escape Fidel."

"And what did they get in Miami?"

"I know, I know, but they're old and they feel good together."

"A lot of young ones are there, too."

"Yes. There are many of them there in the barrio. They don't call them gusanos in their own barrio."

"They're no better off than they were in Cuba. Many are worse."

"They think they're free."

"Yes," Eloisa agreed.

She looked searchingly at her husband. She never knew for sure if Alfonso had left Cuba just for her and the children—and for Papi, his father. Alfonso could be selfless, deny his own needs. He was capable of that. She knew he thought about Cuba a lot.

He often talked of Fidel and Che. Of the great revolution that rid the country of the dictator Bautista. He loved to tell people about the teaching medal presented to him by Fidel himself, and he liked to impress on anyone who would listen his high opinion of Che's honesty and integrity. He frequently argued with other Cuban exiles, but held onto his beliefs. Suddenly Papi jerked, forcing Eloisa out of her thoughts.

"Habana," Papi said, his voice barely audible. "Habana."

Eloisa looked at Alfonso and frowned. He lowered his eyes.

"Habana," the old man said again, his throat rattling weakly.

"He heard us about Cuba," Eloisa said. "Now he's confusing the two again. He doesn't know what he's saying."

"No," Alfonso said. "He doesn't."

Papi suddenly grew still and his head rolled over towards his right shoulder. Eloisa bent over to check his breathing.

"Call the doctor, Alfonso," she said. "And call Father Reyes."

"Stay with us, Papi," she told the old man when Alfonso was gone. "Don't go yet. We still love you. And the girls will miss you so. You have to get well so you can go to Miami. Your old friends are there. In Little Habana, right?"

She patted his face with the now nearly warm cloth. Looking at his washed out face, Eloisa realized her father-in-law would never see Miami—or Habana—again.

"We should have stayed in Cuba, *abuelito*. At least there you could have died at home. In the land where you were born. Oh, Papi, I miss it so bad sometimes. The family, the city, the mountains."

She took the cloth from Papi's head and wiped away her tears. I mustn't cry, she told herself, this is our life. It's what we've made it.

"But, oh, Papi, I miss you already," she said out loud. "I love you." The old man did not stir.

In a few moments, Eloisa rose and took the cloth to soak it again with cool water. When she came back, Alfonso had returned and stood at the end of the bed. He looked worn and haggard.

"How is he?" he asked softly.

Eloisa shook her head.

"The doctor and the priest will be here soon." Alfonso said.

"Good," Eloisa said without passion.

Alfonso cleared his throat. He moved up beside the bed and touched his father's wrinkled hand. There was no response. Alfonso knelt and briefly hugged the old man. He stood up and put his hands on Eloisa's shoulders. She linked her fingers with his.

"I'll go tell the girls," Alfonso said simply.

"Yes," Eloisa said, looking up at her husband. "Yes."

Drinking the Revolution

When the Nicaraguan technical help group, Nicatec, all finally met at the Hotel Majestic in Mexico City, you could tell right away that Robert Maynard was different from the rest.

The vast majority of activist *internacionalistas* neither smoked, drank, nor for that matter seemed to have sex—and Robert showed up with a cigarette in one hand, quickly had a straight whiskey in the other, and was blatantly flirting with three young Mexican girls at a nearby table. It wasn't that the women and men in this group were particularly prudish, but Robert was clearly not cut from the same leftist cloth.

Around the large table where the Nicatecs sat were Tom Gray, a dark-haired, twenty-ish computer programmer and Mary Dopple, a new-wavy independent journalist, both New Yorkers, forty-something Shannon Mailer, a nurse, and Tilly Parks, another programmer, both from New England. Then came Betty Keeler, a med tech, and Robert, a hydrologist, the two of them from the Berkeley area. The de facto group lead was Sam Brewer, a mid-40s freelance writer from Tempe, Arizona.

Brewer was asked to take over the group when the original lead, an experienced Nicatec volunteer from the base group in Berkeley, fell ill and dropped out of the trip. Brewer had been "volunteered" to take the payroll to the permanent Nicatec staff in Managua. $2500 in cash that he carried in a hurriedly-purchased money belt. He was also asked to do a roll call of the volunteers when they arrived in Mexico City for the flight to San Salvador and then on to Managua.

Brewer was nervous as a cat carrying all that cash and was glad Robert Maynard had appeared when he did. With his staccato, machine gun-fast Spanish and his obvious experience, Robert—or Roberto as everyone soon called him—was an excellent counter to Brewer's poor language skills and limited knowledge of the region and its ways.

"Is—is—is this the whole bunch?" Roberto asked after Brewer's roll call. Roberto's English was just as fast, just as pepper-fired as his Spanish. He spoke as if the speed and the energy of his language would in its accumulative effect somehow save his skin, or perhaps his soul. Possibly in the former case it had.

"That's all on the list," Brewer told him.

"Robert, er, Roberto," Shannon asked, appraising the hydrologist with her head cocked somewhat skeptically to one side, "where did you learn to speak Spanish so...so fast?"

"And so well," Betty added with obvious admiration.

"You really know slang and street Spanish," Tilly nodded at Roberto. "That's not Mexican or Central American Spanish I hear, is it?"

"Colombia." Roberto puffed on a cigarette, winked at the Mexican girls again, signaled the waiter for another drink.

"Ah," Tilly said, as if that explained a lot.

"How did you get there?" Brewer asked, emboldened enough to order himself a Superior beer despite the unseen money choking his waist and the possible disapprobation of most of his newly made friends.

"My mother," Roberto said.

"And?" Shannon prompted.

"My dad was a creep. Class-A jerk. He dumped me and mom up in Richmond when I was fifteen and we never heard from him again."

"Then it was your mother who was..." Shannon suggested.

"Colombian," Roberto filled in. "Right. She decided being with her family down there was better than us trying to make it in California."

"Geez," Tom said.

"Where in Colombia?" Betty asked.

"A place called Calí," Roberto told her. "You might have heard of it."

"Whew," Brewer whistled. "Drug country."

"*Exacto*," Roberto tipped his drink to Brewer. Brewer raised his beer glass in acknowledgement.

"Did you go to an American school down there?" Mary asked.

"Ha. I shoulda been so friggin' lucky."

"You mean?" Tilly raised an eyebrow.

"No," Brewer said.

"*Sí*," Roberto confirmed, "most definitely *sí*. I was dumped flat out into a Colombian high school."

"Zero preparation?" Tom asked incredulously.

"Zero, nada," Roberto sniffed.

"*Díos, mío*," Tilly shook her head.

"*Díos* had very little to do with it," Roberto said.

"Jesus," Brewer said.

"Him neither," Roberto joked. The group laughed.

"Really," Brewer asked, "how did you manage to get through that? You didn't know any Spanish? Nothing about the place? That must have been really tough. I mean hell."

"Hell, indeed," Roberto nodded at Brewer. "On the plus side, I know me some Spanish."

"Down cold," Brewer said.

"*Oralé,*" Roberto said. Brewer didn't know what that meant but he pretended he did.

"Well," Shannon commented, "it must have been a very difficult time for you. But it did prepare you wonderfully for this assignment."

"*Te acuerdo,*" Roberto said. "I couldn't agree with you more."

"Man, I sure envy you the language skills," Brewer said.

"Me, too," Betty agreed.

"Ditto," Tom said.

"Let's get something to eat," Mary put in. "All this talking has made me hungry."

"Great idea," Roberto concurred.

"Why don't we just order here," Betty said. "And we can go over our other histories as well."

"Sounds okay to me," Shannon said. The others all nodded or waved their agreement.

"I'm starved," Tilly said. "Easiest to go ahead and eat here. The food is excellent. We ate here on a trip down to Managua last year."

"That settles it," Roberto said, waving at one of several waiters lurking on the other side of the room. "*Joven. Amigo. Por favor.*"

●　　●　　●

"You actually have success with getting girls through personal ads in the newspaper?" Brewer asked Roberto. "Every time?"

Along with Tom Gray and an older *internacionalista* named Fernando, the men had gathered in a small local bar for beers after their second day of work in Managua.

"No," Roberto explained. "But it works often enough. And it simplifies things."

"Simplifies?" Tom queried.

"Clean. Easy. No complicated relationships." Roberto waved at the waiter for another round of beers.

He pulled out a pack of cigarettes and offered it around the table. When everyone declined, he shook one out for himself, lit it and took a deep, satisfying drag, exhaling smoke into the warm, humid Nicaraguan night air.

Brewer looked through the smoke beyond Roberto at a Nicaraguan woman sitting at a nearby table with a man, presumably her husband. The woman had long brown hair, a solid, sexy body, and a fine-featured Indian face. Aware of Brewer's attention, the woman turned her face in profile and smiled—not at Brewer, but into the space past her male companion. Brewer whistled softly.

"What?" Roberto asked.

"Nothing," Brewer said. "Just a tremendously good looking woman behind you."

"With someone?"

"Naturally."

"Forget it. Don't even think about it."

"Not unless through the personal ads, huh?" Brewer joked.

"Right on," Roberto laughed.

"Still on that?" Fernando said.

"Nah," Roberto said. "Just havin' fun."

"Here's the beers," Brewer said as the waiter arrived with four bottles.

The first time he came to Nicaragua they didn't even have beer in bottles, everything was served from the tap into whatever pitcher or container they had or you could bring with you. The revolution had made some progress despite the U.S. covert war against it.

"And here's to being in Nicaragua again. And to the revolution. To Daniel."

Everyone lifted a bottle and drank. Roberto pulled a pint of whiskey out of his pants pocket and offered it to the others. Only Fernando took a shot. Roberto took the bottle back, wiped the mouth with the back of his hand and drained off a good-sized slug.

"After that storm we flew through out of El Salvador," Tom recalled with a shiver, "I'd say we're lucky to be anywhere."

"No kidding," Brewer said. "That was an experience alright. Kind of a counterpoint to the good luck we were having back in the D.F."

"You mean the Mexico City miracles?" Roberto took a drink of beer and lighting up yet another cigarette.

"Mexico City miracles?" Fernando wondered.

"We had a little patch of good luck right as we were leaving Mexico City," Brewer told the older man. "Some things that pretty much run counter to the classic ugly American's view of what Mexicans are like."

"Good luck, with the exception of the tire blowing out on takeoff," Tom reminded Brewer.

"Yeah, except for that."

"Unsatisfying moment." Roberto blew smoke out his nose.

"Uh ... what were the miracles?" Fernando asked again.

"It wasn't earth shattering or anything like that, but it was pretty cool. First, Tilly dropped her checkbook on the curb around the corner from the Hotel Majestic in the zocalo, and a cabbie nearby ran over and retrieved it for her. Cynics would have expected somebody to just pocket the checkbook and bail out of there."

"Possibly," Fernando said.

"And Betty's deal," Tom reminded Brewer.

"Right. Betty, the youngest one in our group, left a box of medical supplies out in the airport when we went through customs. And sure enough somebody found them and the customs people brought them to us in the waiting area by our gate."

"And I lost my damned ticket," Roberto added.

"They brought that to him at the boarding gate itself," Brewer said.

"Amazing." Roberto recalled the moment.

"Actually, that is pretty remarkable," Fernando said. "There were more of these lucky incidents?"

"One more," Brewer went on. "Mary from our group lost her sunglasses somewhere up in customs and can you imagine they actually brought those to her right on the plane as we were getting seated."

"Given Mexico City's reputation for pickpockets and such, it is a rather enlightening sequence of events," Fernando said.

"Quite so," Roberto imitated Fernando's grave way of speaking. Fernando raised an eyebrow. Roberto took a swig of beer and casually drew on his cigarette.

"We weren't so lucky after that, though," Tom said. "We blew a tire on takeoff from Mexico City and got stuck for hours at the San Salvador airport while they rounded some workers up to get a new tire. They delayed us so long we ended up flying into this godawful electrical storm that lasted almost all the way here."

"Really bad?" Fernando asked, looking at Brewer.

"The worst I've ever been in," Brewer said. "With maybe the exception of a really turbulent flight coming back from Puerto Rico to Miami once."

"Easily my worst," Tom said.

"Still damn lucky if you ask me." Roberto took a quick sip of whiskey.

"We got here safe and sound," Brewer said.

"And we got out of El Salvador before they realized we were a plane load of lefties," Tom laughed.

"Right on, dude." Roberto exchanged high fives with Tom.

"All I know," Brewer added, "is that I was damn happy to see Sandino in his Tom Mix hat at the airport when we landed."

"Me, too," Tom said.

"Shall we have another round, gentlemen?" Fernando asked the group. "On me."

"Damned decent of you, Fernando." Roberto handed the veteran leftist the bottle of whiskey and made a drinking motion with his hand.

"*Viva Nicaragua,*" Brewer raised his beer bottle, checking to see if the pretty Nicaraguan lady saw him. She did but betrayed no interest.

"*Viva,*" the others cheered. "*Viva Nicaragua.*"

•   •   •

At the end of the group's first week in-country, Nicatec sprung for a trip to Matagalpa in the mountainous region north of Managua. They took a bus driven by a talkative ex-Sandinista soldier named Carlos who happily related his war stories to the peace-loving *internacionalistas*.

Matagalpa was a lovely, lushly green, city built in a rolling valley surrounded by thickly wooded tropical hills. In town they dropped off two new Spanish workers from a technical group out of Barcelona and picked up two Witness for Peace people from San Diego.

With the exchanges made, Carlos drove to a cemetery at the edge of town. There the group viewed the grave of Ben Linder, an American killed by U.S.-backed Contra insurgents fighting the Sandinista government.

After the somber graveyard visit, the party went to a coffee co-op in the country outside Matagalpa. The atmosphere there was considerably lighter than at the cemetery. This was the real deal socialist thing, with the people working the farm and sharing in its success or failure. They were welcoming to the visitors and Roberto acted as interpreter for Brewer and Tom as the workers described how the farm operated.

When the day ended, the group returned to their hotel, the Selva Negra, a comfortable place which, by Nicaraguan standards, was extremely well-stocked with food and drink. The hotel consisted of a main building and a number of small bungalows around the grounds, nestled in a thickly forested area. It was a pleasant respite from the poverty and warfare that plagued so much of the small nation.

After supper, Brewer and Tom joined Roberto and Carlos in their cottage and ,with a bottle of rum and several beers for company, settled in for a late night bull session. As he liked to do, Carlos regaled the group with tales of the Sandinista army's triumph over the forces of the hated ex-dictator, the very late Anastasio "Tachito" Somoza Debayle.

Roberto did yeoman's translator duty for Brewer and Tom but the alcohol helped and the men laughed and joked well into the dark night. Sometime before midnight, as they began to wind down, Brewer asked Roberto a question he'd wanted to for several days.

"So," he said, chasing a small shot of rum with a big gulp of beer, "what was it like going to high school in Colombia? I mean new country, new language, what the heck?"

Roberto rubbed the stubble on his chin and shrugged. "Not much to tell," he answered laconically. Carlos cocked his head at the unfamiliar English. "*Me preguntaron sobre mis dias en Colombia,*" Roberto explained. Carlos nodded his head. "They're asking me about my time in Colombia."

"C'mon, Robert," Tom chipped in. "We want to hear it."

"Couldn't have been easy," Brewer commented.

"Not even slightly," Roberto said. "Long version, or short?"

"Your choice," Brewer told him.

"Okay," Roberto said, taking a drink of rum and pouring about another shot's worth directly into a glass of beer. He took a slug of that, too, and then lit up a smoke. "You can imagine the Colombian kids weren't all that keen on having a *yanquí* show up out of nowhere. The dudes especially didn't like it. The first time I tried to talk to a girl, I got my butt beat—and good."

"Her beau?" Brewer asked.

"No, man," Roberto laughed. "His *guardaespada*; his bodyguard."

"Bodyguard?" Tom said incredulously.

"Dudes, the schools were just like the rest of Colombia. If you had money or power, somebody else did everything else for you except go to the bathroom."

"How long did this go on?" Brewer asked.

"Months. Until I started picking up on the lingo and figured out who to hang with and who to avoid."

"Did you have a lot of fights?" Tom wondered.

"Lots. I probably lost three or four to each one I won."

"Ow," Tom cringed.

"What finally turned it around for you?" Brewer asked. "I mean, if it ever really did?"

"Oh, it did, alright."

"What happened?"

"Well, after about six or seven weeks I started to get the Spanish. I guess I'd heard more of it than I thought I had from my mom and one day it just sort of came to me. I started talking, talking real fast, as fast as I could to show them I knew their crappy language. Then I got me a girlfriend. That's how you really learn Spanish."

"That did it, huh?" Brewer said. "Then you were in. No more fights or stuff."

"Not quite. I had one more big one."

"Who with?"

"One of the main dude's tough boys."

"You whipped him?"

"I beat him, but it was worse than that."

"What do you mean?"

"I had started carrying a pocketknife after a few beatings," Roberto explained. "And finally I made a choice: die or stop the bull once and for all."

"You cut this guy?" Brewer asked.

"I dropped him several times with punches but he wouldn't stay down. Then he came up with a blade and I pulled mine. He put this scar on my arm," Roberto paused to show everyone the white stripe of dead skin on the back of his left forearm. "But I got mad and nailed him hard. Cut across his chin, his arm, his side. I was ready to kill him when his boss, his *jefe*, stepped in."

"Wow," Tom whistled.

"After that I was square with the crowd. No more big run-ins. Some minor stuff, that's all. The main dude wanted me to be his bodyguard, then, but I said no. I was left alone pretty much from then on. After high school, my mom moved us back to Berkeley—I'd been hanging with another bunch of pretty rough characters, drinking and running hard. She thought I was developing a drinking habit."

With a laugh, Roberto ended his story by draining the rest of the rum and helping himself to what beer remained in both Tom's and Brewer's glasses.

"But you can see I don't," he belched. Carlos laughed when Roberto explained the last part.

"Qué historia," the chofer said, *"qué historia."*

"What a history is right," Roberto said, "*qué historia* indeed."

• • •

At group breakfast next morning in the Selva Negra's large, bright restaurant, all of the late night crew was hung over and subdued except Roberto. He happily sipped whiskey from a flask he carried in his coat pocket into his café con leche and seemed in great spirits. Brewer and Tom barely got their food down under the slightly disapproving glances of the other group members.

By mid- to late-morning, however, when the bus pulled out, the group was back to normal and ready for whatever the day had in store. Or so they may have thought. First stop of the day was a visit in Matagalpa with the Mothers of Heroes and Martyrs— ladies who had lost sons in the current war against the Contras.

To Brewer's utter horror, when the Nicatec group arrived at the little hall to meet the mothers of the dead soldiers, the women gave them a standing ovation. This little group of international workers, whose worst recent suffering would have been some discomfort or the pain of a hangover was applauded by ladies who endured the agonizing death of a child.

Less emotional but perhaps more unsettling for Brewer was the last stop of the day. A brief visit to a state prison some fifty kilometers north of Managua. During the tour of the clean but Spartan facility, Brewer and the other men were taken into a large cell housing some 120 prisoners.

Escorted into the cell by a female Sandinista guard, Brewer and the others hung back, unsure of themselves among so many criminals. Roberto, on the other hand, acted like it was old home week. Rattling his Colombian street Spanish like a linguistic Gatling gun, he was quickly in among the men, laughing, joking, passing out valuable cigarettes.

Brewer watched his new friend with an equal mixture of amazement and admiration. Still, when the guard signaled that the visit was over Brewer was one of the first out the door and quickly reclaimed his seat on the bus for the trip back to Managua.

•   •   •

After the Matagalpa trip, Brewer developed flu-like symptoms. He felt hot and generally weak. He barely ate at supper with the group in their collective home run by a pleasant older couple, Don Francisco and his wife Doña Anita. Later he curled up in a canvas deck chair in an open space beyond the main house. This area was surrounded on all sides with rooms for the boarding international workers. It was warm, airy and filled with tropical plants.

Several parrots hung in cages secured to the ceiling. The colorful birds were often highly animated, loud even to the point of being raucous. While others from the group went looking for evening entertainment, Brewer dug up a copy of *Gorki Park* and settled in for a rest. With fever coming on, he did not know he dozed, even slept, until awakened late by Roberto.

"Brewer, Brewer," Roberto shook his friend gently.

Brewer opened his tired, red eyes, tried to focus. He shook slightly, involuntarily, and knocked his book on the ground by the chair. One of the parrots squawked.

"Damned birds." Roberto tossed a small stick at one of the nearby cages. The bird squawked again, but not so loudly.

"My book," Brewer said from his flu fog. Roberto reached down and retrieved it for him.

"Excellent book." He handed it to the still disoriented Brewer. "It really fills in the parts left out of the movie."

"Roberto?"

"Man, you should go in and go to bed."

"What's happening?"

"It's late, dude. You alright? You don't look so good."

"I don't feel so good," Brewer said, feeling cold. He pulled his shirt close around his chest, then stretched, felt the ache in his bones, yawned again, felt slightly better for just a second. "What are you doing, Roberto? What time is it? Something happen?"

"It's about midnight, dude. I just got back from the street fiesta by the college over here. You know, the UNAM."

"UNAM?"

"The autonomous university a couple of blocks over."

"Oh, how did it go?"

"I don't know, man, I had a little, uh, incident."

"An incident? You had an incident? Sounds like an international diplomacy deal or something."

Brewer coughed. Roberto offered him a shot from his flask. Brewer declined.

"I was just cruising the UNAM party, you see, not doing much. Trolling for chicks, dig? I been there about an hour when I suddenly spot this girl. Cute. Kinda Indian features. She's scoping me and I said, ah-ha. So I move in. And she's sweet. Nice to talk to. Real interested in my water project work down here. You don't suppose she's CIA?" Roberto pronounced it in the Spanish way: see-ah. Brewer shook his head.

"So, anyway, I tell her I'm here for a year and, shoot, then we're really hitting it off."

"Sounds great."

"Yeah, it was, until..."

"Until?"

"Until a couple of punks, they must've known the girl, start kind of following us. The girl got scared and we tried to lose 'em but they stayed on us."

"What did you do?"

"Finally I got tired of it and just stopped, me and the girl. Then I did what I always did in Colombia."

"Yeah."

"I took out my pocketknife and opened it up. Made it real obvious to the two dudes. Showed the blade. Then real slow used it to clean my fingernails."

"Give 'em a message, huh?"

"Exactly."

"Did they get it?"

"Seemed to. They didn't bug us anymore. But it wrecked the deal with the girl."

"That's too bad."

"Uh-huh."

"Well, at least you're okay," Brewer said.

"Yeah, but did I do the right thing, man? I mean, should I have shown the blade?"

"If you had to. You were just protecting yourself."

"It wasn't too much of an uncool thing was it?"

"I don't think so. Maybe some people would, but I don't. Maybe they were dangerous dudes."

"That's right."

"I don't think you did wrong. A man has the right to protect himself."

"Thanks, man," Roberto said, as if Brewer had absolved him of some crime against their shared political ideology. "Thanks a lot."

• • •

The fever came on Brewer hard later that night and he was out of it with the shakes and body pains for several days. He missed two days of work and a good weekend, and he missed Roberto moving out to begin his year's water work project. About the only thing he didn't miss, and he thought it might have been a fever hallucination, was the arrival at the house of an extraordinarily pretty Israeli girl. In his delirium, Brewer mistakenly thought she was a traveling Spanish actress, or some other such heated delusion, the woman's beauty was so great.

By Wednesday of the group's third and last week in-country, Brewer was well, though weak. Due mostly to the fever, he had done little work on the trip and was ready to call it quits.

On the final Friday, the local Nicatec office took Brewer and his group out for a sendoff party. When Roberto dropped by late to say goodbye, Brewer noticed that the permanent Nicatec people, reacting to rumors about his heavy drinking now, viewed Roberto with declining approval.

Some weeks after he returned from Nicaragua, Brewer received a letter from Betty Keeler, the med tech who was also from the Berkeley area. Roberto, the letter informed him, went on an extended bender in Managua. He had been warned, upbraided and finally fired by his Sandinista bosses.

There was no place in the revolution the Sandinistas said, no matter how important personal skills were, for out-of-control drinkers. Roberto was peremptorily sacked and sent back to the United States. Betty reported she had seen Roberto around Berkeley once and although they spoke only briefly, he seemed to be living there as he always had—working, smoking, drinking, finding women through the personal ads.

In a note back to Betty, Brewer expressed some surprise at Roberto's fate but, given his own ineffective time in Nicaragua, was loathe to judge the situation much one way or the other. Sometimes things worked out alright and sometimes they didn't.

The revolution had gone on before any of the *internacionalistas* arrived in the first place and it would go on, or not, with or without them. Brewer asked Betty to remember him to Roberto if she ever saw him again but he never heard anything more from either of them.

The Nicatec trip was Brewer's last to Nicaragua and eventually he lost all contact with his new Nicatec friends. As for the revolution, it did go on, of course—at least in some fashion—and it did so on its own merits, or lack thereof.

Not even skillful foreign workers like Shannon Mailer and Tilly Parks would guide Nicaragua's future. Nor would ill-prepared fellow travelers like Sam Brewer or fast-talking, hard-drinking marginalized figures like Robert Maynard lead it. No, the Nicaraguan people would decide their own destiny. It was up to them. It was in their own hands.

A Near Love Story

Long Distance Call

They took the ten-thirty hydrofoil from Playa del Carmen to Cozumel. She sat next to the window staring out at the sea they bounced over. He sat next to her on the aisle, quietly looking at her profile. Although she was nearly twenty years his junior, she had a grown quality about her, a kind of mature serenity that always surprised him. There was a melancholy side to her that belied her age and her considerable early success. Feeling his gaze on her, she turned briefly and gave him a little smile. A smile all the sadder to him for her obvious effort to make it seem kind and offhand. She turned back to the window but he continued looking at her.

She had a lovely profile, from her strong jawline and slightly pouty mouth to her round, reddish cheeks and button nose. From her high cheekbones and sparkling, intelligent green eyes to her forehead and curly brown hair that fell gently down to her collar. When he looked at her this way, it felt as if he could see into her soul—a cool and beautiful place—and he could not imagine why she was with him, but he didn't care. It was enough just to be with her. To have her turn that smile on him, those sad wonderful eyes.

They spent two days in Playa del Carmen and two lovely evenings. Evenings strolling Playa's sandy little streets, stopping at touristy outdoor restaurants for tacos and pizza and beer. During the days they went for long walks on the beach and when she had wanted, needed to be alone, he let her go.

If he had learned anything in his life, it was to give your partner all the freedom they required. Including the freedom never to come back. To leave with another lover, to go from you forever. That pain would be almost unendurable he knew, but when you loved with all of your being, you would do whatever the object of your love needed. You would not make yourself a slave and you would not be a fool for long, but you would let that person do what they had to do.

She looked at him again and smiled. He took her hand, gently linking his fingers with hers, transmitting as much affection as he could by touch alone. She squeezed his hand and although she then turned away to the window, he felt that his heart would explode from the intensity of his love for her.

It reminded him of the first couple of times he had seen her, when he had stood at the back of the crowd, anonymous, already in love, not yet able to reach her on her level, listening to that overwhelmingly beautiful voice. He felt, as he did now, that his heart would explode from love for her. That his spirit, trapped in the melancholia of failed creativity, would connect to hers in some transcendent way.

Transcendent. Soul.

Those were words, ideas that he didn't even believe in. Such was the power of her spirit—yet another concept he didn't accept—that she lifted him above his materialistic humanism. He believed in nothing—not in god, nor soul, nor spirit, nor love unending. Yet she was the embodiment of all those things. If they had ever existed in a person, they existed in her. He sometimes joked that the religious songs she sang were not just the culmination of two thousand years of Christianity, but the whole point of it. It had all happened, the martyrdoms, the slaughters, the great works of belief and the horrible acts of faith, just so that this most beautiful of voices could sing about it.

And for all that and for all his love for her and her own affection, perhaps love, for him, she was not happy. She had come to fame too soon, too early. The pressures on her were enormous and she frequently felt imprisoned by her own success, by the demands of her public, her art. He wanted desperately to relieve her of that burden, to find a way to remove those extraneous forces from her life so that she might live for and fully love the art she produced with her instrument, her magnificent voice.

No one was more aware than he what an unusual couple they were. She was young, pretty, spiritual in a down-to-earth way, magically talented. He was middle-aged, not very good looking, a self-proclaimed agnostic leaning toward atheism with a despairing existential perspective, a writer of pedestrian talent. Yet his love for her lifted him above the mundane failure of his own life and transformed him from a hopeless, helpless egotist to what he believed was a far better man, one who was outer directed, self-sacrificing—caring.

He was devoted to her and when he was with her she was the center of all he knew. His goal was to make her content, happy if possible, and he tried to stay focused on that goal. Some might say he had lost himself in her, but he knew he had found himself there instead. Because she wasn't just anybody. She was a true—a great—artist. To serve her was to serve art. Art embodied in a beautiful young woman. To him, nothing could surpass that.

Now, nearing Cozumel, he continued to hold her hand and look at the side of her face, tracing it, trying to memorize every line and angle of her jaw and chin and lips. She turned towards him, the corners of her eyes crinkling in a smile. He leaned close to her.

"I love you," he whispered.

She bent toward him, kissed him lightly on the cheek, then rested her head against the side of his. He reached over and stroked her thick hair. He could feel her tiredness, the soul weariness that her exhausting schedule produced in her. He touched her cheek, feeling its softness, and so close to her, breathed in the delicate odor of her hair and body. He turned in his seat so that he could move his face closer to hers. She looked at him without expression and he kissed her gently on the lips. She returned his kiss, then turned away again to look out at the sea. He looked straight ahead but held tightly to her hand.

On the dock at Cozumel they walked off the ferry together, not holding hands but side by side. They were about to look for a taxi when she remembered she left a day bag on the ferry.

"I'll get it," he said, immediately moving back towards the boat. She reached out and held his arm.

"No, it's okay," she said. "It's nothing important. There's nothing in it worth anything."

"I'll get it," he repeated, pulling away from her. "I'll be right back."

He strode away purposefully. She walked on through the milling crowd. Just before he re-entered the ferry, he looked for her but could no longer see her. He hurried into the ferry without looking back.

•   •   •

They were stretched out on hotel beach chairs sunbathing. He had drunk more beer than they both knew he should and was now distant and melancholy. She knew the mood. He tried not to be that way, she honestly believed, and he seldom was, but at odd times he seemed unable to stop and would drink himself away from her. She suspected he was preparing himself for when she would no longer be there.

Watching him—silent, moody, sunk in his own pain—she felt the great tiredness that had plagued her since even before the last tour had begun. She was so very tired. Tired of the demands upon her from family, career, fans, and from him.

She smiled remembering the first time they met, such a short time ago really. His agent had called her agent and on the morning before a concert the four of them got together at her hotel. His agent introduced him as a screenwriter and novelist, "a big fan."

He was shy and nervous at first, but then loosened up and she thought he was clever and charming, funny. That was what she liked best. He made her laugh, made her feel at ease. And he was so obviously taken with her. From the very beginning. She teased him back and flirted a little, not meanly. Saw that beneath the jokes and fan talk, he really was interested in her, and in her career.

Later they walked in a nearby park and his praise of her made her feel happier than she had in months. They ate salads at a little restaurant and she invited him to watch that night's show from backstage.

The band was very tight and she sang with a feeling missing since the start of the tour. Towards the end of the show she glanced into the wings and he was there holding up a big sign requesting the song she always liked to sing most. She laughed and smiled at him, wondering if that was his favorite song, too or if somebody in the crew had put him up to it. He gave her a little wave and winked and she sang the song better than she had since she recorded it, remembering how beautiful it was, and how sad.

After the show he waited patiently to congratulate her, stayed until all the fans, musicians, and other hangers-on were gone. He appeared again at her hotel room, holding a single red rose and a CD that he made her autograph against her objections. They talked well into the early morning and he told her he believed he was in love with her even though they didn't know each other very well yet.

He told her she was very, very special—overwhelming her by saying she was among the elite artists, those who would live for the ages. He apologized for being so "forward," but, he said she was too special—a word he used a lot—not to be told so. Just before dawn he excused himself, knew she had a rough schedule to keep, and with a gentle handshake, left. When he was gone, she lay on her back on the bed and laughed out loud for joy.

During the rest of the tour he appeared off and on, always when she least expected him, and they saw each other when they could—eventually nearly all the time. He became a buffer for her, absorbing the anxiety producing tensions between her and her manager, her fans, her band members, anyone who could distract her from her music, and they had a wonderful four months together.

Then she took him home, against his will, to meet her family. Her dad, brothers, and sister tolerated him, even grudgingly liked him. Her mother did not.

"He's older than I am," her mother said. "He could be your father. How did we go wrong with you? Does he... well, does he have his own money?"

She laughed bitterly at the memory. Somehow, her mother's attitude spread to her manager, her band, and then although she fought it, to herself. And he changed. He became defensive, held on now where he hadn't before, forced that which he wanted most away from him. He seemed old and although she chided herself for such an attitude, she began to notice younger men again, to think about her own personal future—a home, a family, all the things they would not likely have together.

She looked at him, nearly passed out on his beach chair, and a great swelling of emotion surged within her. She fought back tears. She had loved him and he had been wonderful for her, for a while. But she couldn't love him anymore and it made her immeasurably sad. It was all too difficult now, his love would cost her too much.

"Damn it," she said, surprised by her own rare swearing.

He didn't seem to hear or at least didn't look over. She leaned back in the chair and hid her face with a beach towel. It felt dark and simple under there and fit her mood perfectly.

• • •

That evening, sunburned and sober, he was himself again. Solicitous, kind, funny. She hugged him tightly when they entered the hotel restaurant and he made a production of getting her seated. To her amusement, he ordered their meals in Spanish and carried on happily with the restaurant help. She watched him, her eyes crinkled from the smile that he said made her the prettiest woman he'd ever seen. So pretty he said, in his typical, fanciful writer's way, she would melt the heart of the hardest man on earth.

In his extravagance, he spilled water on the white peasant pants he'd bought that afternoon and she laughed out loud at the stain that made him look like he'd peed his pants. He laughed to see her laugh and they had kissed across the table and smiled at each other a lot over their plates of rice and enchiladas. He had just ordered them dessert when the long distance call came.

"Who in the world could that be?" She saw the curtain of self-protection drop over and dull the sparkle that had returned to his eyes. "I didn't think anybody knew where we were."

"It's probably your mother," he said tonelessly.

She excused herself and checked her phone. It was her manager.

"No, Harry." She turned away to speak. "I told you no before we left."

He could hear the voice on the other end of her phone but could not make out the words.

"The difference," she said, "is that the record company doesn't care about me. Harry, just the money I make for them—yes, he does—I know you do, too—How can I come back right now—Why? —They could get someone else—all right, all right."

The Interview

He tried hard not to show how nervous he was. When her manager introduced them, though, he awkwardly shifted the small, stuffed briefcase he carried from his left to right hand, nearly dropping it. Feeling foolish he reached out and shook her hand. It was firm but smooth, her grip relaxed and comfortable. He wanted to keep holding her hand but forced himself to let go so that she wouldn't think he was any more of an idiot than he already felt himself to be.

"I'll let you two talk then," her manager said.

He gave the manager an appreciative smile and felt a pair of light green eyes appraising him. With great effort he composed himself and turned back to face her. She was smiling at him.

"Thank you for letting me share some of your time." He looked briefly into those lovely eyes. "I know you have a busy schedule."

She smiled again and he was temporarily silenced by the enormous absurdity of the situation he had placed himself—and her—in. How could he possibly expect to convey to her in a short conversation what he'd been thinking about her for years. Without, that is, sounding like a lunatic and sending her scrambling for the safety of her entourage. But she rescued him, just as he had foreseen in one of myriad variations of the current scene he had projected in his past fantasies about meeting her.

"What kind of writing do you do?" she asked in a sweet voice, one more down-to-earth than it sounded on the many television interviews of her he had watched. "Are you a reporter?"

"Oh, no." He was quick to disassociate himself from the written word paparazzi. "I write, uh, fiction. Novels and stuff like that."

"And stuff like that," she echoed, eyes crinkling in a smile that devastated him.

Was she making fun of him, being ironic? He couldn't tell and didn't care. He was in a little bit of a daze.

"Would I have heard of them?"

"Heard of what?"

"Your book, or books, or whatever you write."

"What … uh, oh, no, I'm sure not. I'm not very well known."

She laughed a small laugh, cute and lilting. He immediately knew with her he would make a complete fool of himself. He laughed happily.

"I have a couple of books out, but they only sold enough to keep the publishers from coming after me for my blood."

She laughed the laugh again. "What are they about?"

"About? Oh, uh, you know, this and that."

"Very mysterious."

"I'm sorry. I'm being dense. I'm not comfortable talking about my poor little writings, especially when I'm with a real artist. It seems a bit silly."

"I'm sure you're wrong. I bet they're good, whatever they're about."

"Well…,"

"Do you write poetry, too?"

"No, no poetry. Well, I used to. Every now and then I write a poem if the mood strikes me. But, no, I write mostly fiction."

"That's wonderful. What's your inspiration?"

"I don't really think about inspiration."

"No?"

"No."

"What is it then that drives you?"

"Over the years," he recounted, hoping he wasn't going to come off like the egocentric pontificator his friends sometimes called him, "I've written for lots of reasons. For money, for acclaim, literary pretensions, you name it. I've gone through all the stages and more. I simply write because it's what I do. Good, bad or indifferent. I seem compelled to do it, so I do. As for what it's about—I guess it's basically realistic writing, with a sociological bent. I don't really know for sure."

"That sounds very deep," she said.

"It's deep alright. Right up to the hip boots." She laughed happily and shook her head.

"So if you're not a reporter, then why did my manager call this an interview?"

"I guess it was sort of my only way to get to meet you without you thinking I was a crazed stalker kind of fan. I wanted to meet you on something like equal ground. You know, artist to artist. If you'll forgive me putting myself in your category."

"Goodness, you have an awfully low opinion of yourself."

"Anyway, what I would like to do, if it isn't too stupid, is give you a copy of my latest book."

"Why, that would be really nice."

"I don't know if it's the kind of book you would even like, but it's all I have to give to thank you for your great gift and work."

"That's very kind, thank you."

He took a hardbound copy of the book from his briefcase and handed it to her. She immediately opened it and thumbed through the pages slowly.

"Will you sign it for me?" she asked, pushing the book back towards him.

"You're kidding, right?"

"No, please. Sign it."

"For heaven's sake." He reached in his shirt pocket for a pen. While he was signing the book, her manager appeared.

"I'm sorry to interrupt, Lisa, but there are some folks waiting to see you. Mr. Finerty, you'll forgive us."

"Oh … sure." Finerty handed the book back to Lisa.

"Look, Brian, Mr. Finerty gave me a copy of his new novel."

"Jim. Please, call me Jim."

"Well, Jim," Brian said, "I really do have to whisk her away."

"Of course." Finerty rose as Lisa stood. "Thank you so much for your time. It was really nice of you."

"Thank you." Lisa held up the book.

"Well, goodbye." He nodded to Brian and shook Lisa's hand.

"Goodbye," she said, "I enjoyed our lunch."

"Me, too," Finerty said, "it was my pleasure."

As Lisa and Brian walked away through the restaurant, Finerty remained at the table, watching them, or her, walk away. At the front door, Lisa surprised him when she turned and walked back towards him.

"Are you coming to the concert tonight?"

"I was hoping to."

"Would you like to watch from backstage? You could hang with Brian."

"Oh my, yes, that would be fantastic."

"Okay. Come a little early and look for me or Brian. We'll get you a pass."

"I will. Thank you."

She waved goodbye and hurried off. Finerty grabbed his ragged briefcase and made his way to the cashier.

"Yes," he said under his breath as he bounced along. "Yes."

• • •

After the concert, which garnered three encores, Finerty remained backstage among but not part of the post-show excitement. The band laughed and joked, wiped sweat from their hands and faces, met with adoring fans.

Finerty waited quietly to one side of the hubbub and watched Lisa and the band work the die-hards, the hangers-on, the devoted followers. He patiently observed the interaction for nearly three-quarters of an hour in hopes of talking to Lisa again. When it looked like she would never get away, he wound his way towards the back door of the theatre, where he'd been let in earlier. Just as he was about to step outside a soft voice stopped him.

"Were you going to leave without saying goodbye?"

"Uh ... I."

"That wasn't very nice of you." Lisa affected a stern attitude towards him.

"I'm sorry."

"I'm just teasing, you know," she laughed.

"Oh, jeez, I thought I had screwed up."

"Now it's my turn to say I'm sorry."

"Aah, no way. I didn't think you were going to ever get free."

"It's an occupational hazard."

"I'm getting it now.

"Do you really have to go?"

"I probably should. You look awfully busy. But thanks a lot. The show was terrific, as always. You sounded great."

"Really? I thought I was pretty off tonight."

"Are you kidding me?" he laughed. "Off? Not likely. I don't think that's possible."

"Well, thank you. How sweet of you to say."

"Absolute truth."

"How kind...,"

"C'mon, Lisa, hon," Brian interrupted breathlessly. He had a TV reporter and cameraman in tow. "These folks are from the local TV station. They want to talk to you."

Whisking Lisa up, Brian maneuvered her away from Finerty and over to an empty corner. Finerty watched from afar, prepared to leave. As he walked towards the back door once more, Lisa broke from the interview and ran over to him. She produced a small card and a pen, wrote quickly on back of the card, then handed it to Finerty.

"What?"

"Call me," she mouthed silently. Finerty was dumbfounded. "Call me," she said out loud this time, "tomorrow."

"Uh ... what time?"

"Surprise me, but not too early."

"No, no," Finerty said to her retreating figure. "Not too early."

Lisa ran back to her interview and Finerty staggered out of the theatre into the cool evening air. There were still a few show-goers out on the sidewalk but he passed them by, barely aware other people existed on the planet.

"My, God," he said out loud, not knowing or caring if anyone heard him or not. "I cannot believe this is happening to me."

Some of the young people he walked by laughed at the crazy man talking to himself, but Finerty didn't notice. He was oblivious to it all, save Lisa. She had given him her phone number and told him to call the next day. As far as he was concerned, that made tomorrow the only thing that meant anything at all. It was the only thing that played in his head, everything else was just background noise.

Come Back

He returned to the States to finish the novel the trip to the Yucatan interrupted. He struggled with the book, hoped it would be the one to put him over the top, doubted it would. To break the dreary hard work, he took his work to a favorite outdoor restaurant, sat in the air under an awning, sipped on beer, wrote, and pretended he was Ernest Hemingway in Paris in the 1920s. As he struggled with a particularly difficult passage, a shadow suddenly blocked the light on his manuscript. A little annoyed, he looked up and it was her.

"Hi." She smiled in that little girl way he could not resist. "Mind if I join you?"

He laid his pencil on the manuscript and motioned for her to sit down. They looked at each other for a moment, awkwardly shifting in their seats.

"You look great." He wished he didn't always have to compliment her the minute he saw her.

"So do you." A waiter appeared to take her order but she didn't want anything.

"I thought you were still on tour."

"I am, we're playing in Santa Fe tomorrow night."

"How's it going?"

"Great. The band misses you."

"I'm sure."

"Are you finally getting a chance to finish your book?"

"How did you find me here? I didn't tell anybody where I was."

"I had my agent call your agent," she grinned. "Two can play that game, you know."

He smiled at her reference to his original ploy that brought them together. No matter what had passed between them, he would never regret having made that first connection.

"I miss you." She reached her hand across the table.

He placed his hand on top of hers and lightly stroked her smooth skin.

"I don't know what to say," he said out loud, the words catching in his constricting throat.

"Tell me you miss me, too."

"I miss you."

"I brought you a present." She reached in her bag and set a phone on the table between them.

"Really?" he laughed.

"So you can return all those calls I made that you didn't get."

"Sorry. I had no idea."

"That's why I had to call your agent finally. You're a hard man to get in touch with."

"I'm glad you did."

"Me, too."

"How's the tour going, really?"

"Great. Seriously. Nice small places. My favorite."

"They're the best."

"They are."

"Can you stay?" he asked.

"What would our agents say?" she laughed. He tried a weak smile. "Wouldn't I be interrupting your work?"

"You could never interrupt my work."

"Say please," she teased.

"No games," he rejoined. Her smile faded.

"No games."

"I'm not trying to be a jerk here."

"You're never a jerk to me."

"Where are we now?" he asked.

"Let's see," she joked, "Fourth Avenue and..." She stopped when he didn't smile. "We're trying to get back together?"

"How do we do that? What do we do? What do I do?"

"Tell me again why you love me," she said simply, seriously.

"You know why."

"Please, tell me."

"I love you...because even though you always try to minimize yourself, to be a down-to-earth, regular person, you're not. You have an extraordinary gift. You sing with a beauty and sweetness that comes from somewhere deep inside you. From some deeper you, some special you that makes you bigger and greater than the you who lives in the 'regular' world. You're an amazing artist, and whatever it is inside you that makes you so, that's what makes me love you the way I do."

She took his right hand in both of hers. He looked into her eyes, saw the tears there, saw one roll slowly down her cheek. He reached over and wiped it away with his left index finger.

"To me, you're the most beautiful person in the world. Simple as that."

"Will you come back? Back to me."

"Is it what you want? For the long haul? Am I enough?"

She looked at him for a long time without speaking. Unconsciously she rubbed his hand with her fingers, searched his eyes with hers, searching, he felt, for his very soul.

"I'm exactly what you see in front of you," he said, not breaking eye contact. "There's nothing else. I can't be anybody else but who I am."

She continued to plumb his soul with her eyes for a few moments more, then she shook her head up and down slowly. He leaned forward and kissed her on the cheek.

"Will you come back with me?" she asked again, this time dry-eyed.

"Yes," he smiled. "If you want me to."

"Yes," she said softly, taking both his hands in hers. "Yes, I do."

At a Station on the Metro

"What do you think?" Connor Owens asked Jake Mitchell for the third time that sunny, bright Friday morning. It was the last workday of their two-week trip to the Hiraki plant outside Tokyo. "You think Kimiko would go out with me?"

Jake started to climb out of the giant color printer they were working on, but instead removed three Phillips screws on a slender metal strip near the transfer station of the printer. Using a clean cloth, he wiped down the metal strip and laid it on a work table by the printer next to several other parts he had removed.

"Dude," he finally told Connor, "how the heck should I know. I'm married, remember? Kimiko's your deal, man."

"Yeah, but, she's dynamite, man. Even if you're married you can see that. You think she digs me?"

"Listen to me." Jake shook his head. "Kimiko is super sweet and very pretty. I'm not blind. But you're not hearing me. I'm not interested in what she thinks of me or you. That's your department. All I want to do is get back home to see Marcy and the kids."

"Oh, man. Here she comes. Jeez, look at her."

Jake groaned. "Get a grip."

Kimiko served as the American engineers' translator and she was pretty. Her shiny, dark black hair fell to her shoulders, accentuating her high Asian cheekbones, almond-shaped brown eyes, and full, pleasant mouth. She was a little taller than the average Japanese woman with a fine, athletic build.

"Good morning, Connor-san. Jake-san."

"Good morning, Kimiko-san." Jake popped out of the printer for a moment.

"Hey, Kimi," Connor said, far too familiarly for Jake's taste. "How you doin'?"

"I'm fine, Connor-san." Kimiko ignored Connors' breach of Japanese social etiquette. If the Japanese were anything, they were respectful and polite. "How is your work coming along?"

"We're doin' great."

"How about you, Jake-san?"

"We're getting there." Jake removed a plastic piece from inside the machine. "We should have the conversion done in a few hours. We'll be finished by this afternoon, I'm sure."

"Have you seen Matsui-san and the others yet this morning?"

"Ha," Connor laughed.

Jake gave his buddy a quick look. He didn't think it was a good idea to let Kimiko in on the series of evenings out they'd been having with their co-workers.

Connor and Jake lifted weights and were body builders. They were energetic, fresh-faced and friendly. Their Japanese co-workers, all Hiraki engineers, looked at them as though they were part of some American genetic experiment. Watanabe, a squat, officious by-the-book man, Tanaka, a young, rail-thin new-hire, and Matsui, an older and highly deferential Hiraki lifer, were in complete awe of the young *gaijin*.

"I think they're over in another lab."

In fact, Jake hadn't seen them yet this morning. He couldn't imagine they were late to work. That was simply not allowed in the Japanese workplace.

"I'm sure they'll be around any time now."

"Are we still on for this evening, Kimi?" Connor asked.

"We are still on, Connor-san."

Connor pointed an index finger at her and smiled. Kimiko blushed and almost laughed. Jake shook his head again. When it came to pretty women, Connor was completely incorrigible.

•   •   •

Jake and Connor, working steadily, completed the printer conversion just before four-thirty in the afternoon. All that stood between them and a final night among the bright lights of Tokyo was wrapping up some paperwork and saying goodbye to their host engineers.

The three Hiraki men arrived at the lab mid-morning, seemingly none the worse for the previous evening's outing. They stood nearby as the young Americans completed their work, taking notes and making polite comments and suggestions. Connor and Jake teased their hosts about being late at the lab, but Matsui-san informed them in his serious manner that they had attended a meeting with their manager and were at work punctually as always.

"Sure you did," Connor joked. "You guys were hiding out in some other lab with hangovers."

"No, no, Connor-san." Matsui-san shook his head. "We would never do such a thing. No, no."

"Of course not," Jake smiled. "Not Hiraki men."

After cleaning up the work area and collected their tools, it was time for Jake and Connor to say goodbye. Bowing deeply over and over, the five men said a formal farewell and shook hands somberly.

"It was great working with you fellows again," Jake said.

"It is Hiraki's pleasure to have worked with the fine

Americans," Matsui-san said for his co-workers. "We would be pleased you return again."

"Thank you." Jake bowed again.

Kimiko reappeared to spirit the Americans off. With a wave, Jake and Connor headed out of the plant, their lovely young guide leading the way.

• • •

By the time the two Americans returned to their hotel and packed for the following day's flight, it was six-thirty. It was nearly dark, and the fine bright day slowly gave way to a cool, rainy evening. They caught a cab to the train station, where they found Kimiko already waiting for them on the platform, clad in a smart, black leather jacket.

"Lookin' great, Kimiko," Connor said as soon as he saw her in the crowd of humanity at the edge of the platform steps.

Jake rolled his eyes.

"Hello, friends," Kimiko smiled. "Are we ready to see Tokyo's nightlife?"

"You bet." Connor edged up next to her. She blushed and looked down at her feet.

"This'll be fun," Jake added. "It's good to get that conversion done."

"I think you miss your family, Jake-san," Kimiko said.

"I do."

"I can't wait to get to Tokyo," Connor said. "Are you ready for some fun, Kimiko? We're gonna have a blast."

"Easy, tiger," Jake laughed.

Kimiko giggled and averted her eyes from Connor's rapt admiration. "Let's move up closer to the edge of the floor here. We catch our train better that way."

"All right," Jake said.

Weaving through the crowd, the threesome made their way to the edge of the platform and settled in to wait. While Jake daydreamed about home and family, Connor kept up an easy banter with Kimiko. Their laughter and chatter barely registered in the older man's ears. Imagining a trip to the park back home with his wife and kids, it took him a few seconds to notice the commotion. Across the tracks, on the platform directly across the way, something was happening.

Suddenly, a man tripped and then fell off the platform onto the ground beside the tracks.

"Jake," Connor yelled. "Look. Over there."

"Oh, my goodness," Kimiko exclaimed.

"Man," Jake said. "That guy fell on the tracks."

The man appeared to be unhurt but when he staggered back to his feet, Jake could see he was too short to reach up and pull himself back onto the platform. People in the crowd bent over to help, but to no avail. Absorbing the scene's potential for disaster, Jake acted on impulse.

He ripped off his jacket and leapt to the tracks below. In an unthinking heartbeat, he raced toward the man who still tried to get back up on the platform. In a flash, he cleared one set of rails, then another. He moved fast, but there seemed to be no end to the tracks. Tracks for the fast trains—the ones that didn't stop at the station—were in the center. Those trains traveled at nearly bullet train speed.

"Oh, crap," Jake cursed.

Adrenalin pumping, Jake stormed across the center rails faster than he had run since he was a cross-country man at Florida State. He shot over the remaining tracks and quickly reached the other side of the station. The Japanese man still stood there, struggling vainly to reach for the platform. In one powerful sweeping motion, Jake grabbed him and tossed him up, over, and onto the ledge above. It was amazing at how light the man was—like tossing a child's rag doll

The shocked man cried out and rolled across the concrete floor of the platform. Jake quickly pulled himself to safety.

When he landed on the platform, he finally realized what he had done.

My God, he thought. *I could've been killed. I've freaked out everybody in the entire station. And I'm on the wrong side of the tracks. I'm going to miss my train.*

With a cry of his own, Jake bolted across the platform, the Japanese clearing a path before him as if he were the incarnation of the force that had parted the Red Sea.

As he roared past the stunned workers, Jake briefly made eye contact with a taller, dignified local man who frowned at him, the fleeing *gaijin*. He almost stopped to apologize but raced on, instead, down the stairs to the tunnel heading back to his own platform.

His knees wobbled as he churned up the steps to where Connor and Kimiko awaited him, still rooted to the spot they'd been when Jake made his great leap of abandon. They stared at him wide-eyed and slack-jawed as Jake regained his composure. Calmly picking up his jacket, he brushed it off carefully, and casually put it back on. He ran a hand through his short hair and turned to face his companions.

"What?"

"Dude!" Connor exclaimed. "What the hell was that?"

"Oh, Jake-san." Kimiko shuffled nervously. Everyone on both platforms looked at them.

"Man," Connor said, "you just jumped on the tracks and ran over and threw that guy back on the platform."

"Jake-san," Kimiko said, "I think we need to go soon."

"Uh, sure," Jake concurred, but he didn't see how they could go any sooner than when the train actually got there.

"Oh, dear," Kimiko said. "I think the trains are all stopping."

"Uh-oh," Connor groaned.

Jake concentrated on his surroundings. Something big was missing. It was sound. Sound was missing. There was no sound in the busy station. The trains had stopped.

"Whoa," he said.

"What were you thinking?" Connor asked incredulously, wildly, stepping up close to Jake. "You could've got killed with that freako hero shit. What were you doing? You're unbelievable, dude. You're a hero. You're a mad freak. Beer's on me, dude. Holy crap."

"Something's happening over there, Jake-san." Kimiko spoke before Jake formulated a response to Connor's crazed colloquy.

"Uh, oh," Connor groaned again.

Jake looked across the tracks to the other platform. Something was definitely happening. Dark uniformed Japanese police moved through the crowd, gesturing.

"I'm going to jail," he said quietly to himself. "I'm going to rot in a Japanese prison forever."

"Look." Kimiko indicated the platform across the tracks.

They looked over and saw the taller, dignified man who had frowned at him during his mad scamper across the other platform. The man pointed towards them. Then, in a moment of preternatural quiet in a place normally very loud, everyone heard the man call out in English so perfect he could have passed for an American himself.

"That's him. That's the one." He pointed over at Jake. "That American over there."

Thanks a lot, Jake wanted to call out, but held his tongue.

"Oh, hell," Connor said. "Now we've had it."

"Relax, dude," he said—but he meant it for himself.

"Jake-san," Kimiko said, "those are the police. They are coming over here."

"I'm hip."

The police disappeared down the same steps he had run down himself just moments—or was it an eternity—ago.

In seconds, the police surrounded them, chattering and gesticulating. Kimiko interpreted as fast as she could, but in her own terror only caught words and phrases. Jake and Connor had no idea what was happening.

Suddenly a hard-faced officer, apparently the highest ranking one of the group, stepped forward. He waved his hand for silence. The chattering stopped. Everyone stood in place. Jake thought again of Japanese prisons and dungeons and the family he would never see again.

The man in command—maybe a sergeant or lieutenant from the markings on his uniform and hat—barked something. Kimiko answered, bowing low in deference to the man's rank and authority. The man dismissed her with an imperious wave of the hand and spoke directly to Jake—in heavily-accented English.

"You," the man said forcefully. "Come with us."

The other officers herded the two Americans, with Kimiko tagging along behind, down the platform steps and into a small building at the bottom of the stairs. Inside, sitting on a wooden chair, was the little man Jake had rescued. He did not look up.

The police pointed at another chair beside the man. Jake took it. He knew this was hardly the time to be too sensitive about his right as an American to not be pushed around.

The police shouted again, but only at the Japanese man, clearly berating him. The man never looked up, answered them quietly, bowed frequently

"What are they doing?" Jake whispered to Kimiko. "Why—"

"Please be quiet, Jake-san." Kimiko said. The head officer glanced at them.

"Am I going to jail?"

"Sshh." Kimiko put a finger to her lips.

The grilling of the little man continued. The police pointed repeatedly at a big board to one side of the little room with an uncountable number of red lights. The train schedule Jake guessed. The little man spoke softly and bowed. He never looked up. Finally, when it seemed the police had their fill of yelling at the man, the lead officer spoke to Kimiko who translated for Jake.

"Jake-san," she said slowly and precisely, "the man you threw onto the platform says he is grateful for your attention to his health. He is in your debt for your actions and will repay you."

Still not lifting his head, the man handed a brochure to Jake. Kimiko explained the man owned a number of taxis in Tokyo and that he, Jake, could have all the free rides he ever wanted by calling the number listed at the bottom of the brochure.

"Oh," Jake said, not sure what to make of this development. "That's nice. Thank you very much."

He spoke directly to the man, but the man did not look up and even turned slightly away. The lead police officer spoke again, his voice as authoritarian as ever.

"What did he say that time, Kimiko-san?"

"He said you should use this man's taxicabs, Jake-san."

"Oh," Jake began, "but we're—"

"Please," the police official cut Jake off, spoke again in English. "Hear me."

"Um, yes, sir."

"Japan's citizens," the officer said with a precise bow, "are happy of the actions of a foreigner in stopping our citizen from maybe harm. But in future," he paused to make his final point clear, "please be staying off the tracks of Japan."

"We're free to go?" Jake looked at Kimiko to see if he had understood correctly.

"We can go."

"We're outta here," Connor said, the first words he'd uttered since they were herded into the little building.

Jake stood and bowed low to the little man he'd rescued and to the police. "I am—"

Kimiko grabbed his arm and Connor's and drug the two men towards the door of the little building and the cool evening air awaiting them outside.

"We go now," she said. "Right now."

•   •   •

The train station episode cast a shadow over Jake and Connor's plans for their last evening in Japan. They went on into Tokyo with Kimiko and hit a few nightspots, but no one seemed up for the excursion anymore.

To Connor's dismay, Kimiko left early, citing weekend plans, and he spent the rest of the evening trying to chat up Japanese girls. When none of them could match Kimiko, he gave up.

The flight home the next day was uneventful. Jake suffered from a rare hangover and Connor read magazines and daydreamed about women he had won and lost. Back at work, the young engineers found that their department had been realigned and that they were assigned to a new printer, one that would restrict their travel to stateside locales.

Occasionally at department meetings, someone who had heard of Jake's fateful leap would dredge it up for a joke and ask whether he might "please be staying off the tracks of Japan." That usually got a good laugh and after a while the story became semi-legendary, a part of the department's oral history.

As for Connor and Jake, they had mixed feelings about the whole experience. It had been funny alright, but a little too surreal to enjoy all that much. The unsure moments with the police were more frightening than comic. It did make a darned good yarn around the water cooler or over a brew pub beer, though. Neither of them ever went back to Japan and in the long run, for all the parties concerned, that was probably just as well.

Up from Matagalpa

If Anna Lee Dunn hadn't caught hepatitis in the jungles of Nicaragua, I would have never had the opportunity to know her. I'd seen her around town many times before she went to Central America and she was at every demonstration I was.

Once, on my first trip to Nicaragua, I took a care package to her from her folks in Tucson. Later that trip, we accidentally saw each other on a street beside the pyramid-shaped Hotel Intercontinental in Managua. But until she came back to Tucson to recuperate I never really got to know her.

I was distributing a radical newsletter I wrote called *Con Plomo* at a U.S. Out of Central America rally in Tucson when I ran into Anna Lee. She was in a food line ahead of me.

"Hello," I said.

"Well, hello," she smiled. "It's been a while."

Up close she was even taller than I remembered, and definitely thinner—courtesy of a bout with hepatitis she'd picked up in the mountainous region near Matagalpa where she worked. She had shoulder-length brown hair that she clearly didn't feel like worrying about. It was sort of tousled and covered the sides of her plain, unadorned face. She was not what people would call traditionally pretty, but was very pleasant to talk to. There was an intelligent sparkle in her eyes and she had a pleasantly ironic way of speaking that made her appealing.

"I'm sorry you had to come back this way." I groped for some way of keeping her attention aimed at me.

"I'm just glad to get some good food, to tell you the truth. It's hard to get a lot of stuff down there. But you know that. You've been down twice, right?"

"Right."

I knew what she meant, but being around a real, permanent volunteer to the revolution made me feel like the worst kind of political dilettante, especially compared to her deep commitment. I had been to Nicaragua twice, for three weeks each time, and although I learned a lot, I had accomplished little.

"Remember that time I saw you on the road by the Hotel Intercontinental in Managua?"

"Of course."

I tried to think of something else to say.

"Are you going to the Calero demo next Saturday?" she asked, letting me off the conversational cross upon which I had impaled myself.

"S...sure. I guess I was sort of going to be in it."

"Oh, yeah?"

"Yeah. Are you going to be there?"

"I guess I'm sort of in it, too."

"Cool. I didn't know that."

"Well." She waved to some friends beyond the ramada, signaling the imminent end of our conversation. "I better do some mingling."

"It was nice seeing you again."

"Me, too," she said without a hint of irony. "See you later."

"Later," I said. She walked away. I called after her: "Hope you get to feeling better."

She waved and smiled. I stood in the ramada and watched her walk slowly through the park and join her friends.

• • •

The Saturday demonstration turned out pretty well. Something like four or five hundred people showed up, as many as I'd ever seen at any protest in my time in Tucson. Everyone was there, from hard core lefties to well-off liberal democrats.

We put on an amateurish piece of street theatre in which Anna Lee played a sleazy government official channeling illegal funds to contra chief Calero. I was Calero, even though I had gray hair and a gray beard, and was a scrawny representation of the obese would-be Nicaraguan political boss. I jammed the play money Anna Lee offered me into all my pockets, letting lots of it fall out onto the ground. The crowd ate up our little show.

When the demo was over—there hadn't been too many hitches in it and we hadn't had the typical counter protest—Anna Lee and I and a couple of our mutual friends crossed Broadway to where our cars sat in a dying strip mall parking lot.

"Which one of these is yours?" Anna Lee asked with a wry smile. There was a nice new brown Honda Accord near us, a sporty, late-model red Mustang, and an old, sun-baked, gray Toyota Corolla.

"That's mine." I pointed to the Toyota. Anna Lee's wry smile turned into a laugh.

"I thought all you IBMers drove BMWs. Beamers for Beamers."

"Not everybody," I smiled back at her. "I ain't into that shit."

Our friends suggested going somewhere for an early meal and I said that sounded good to me.

"I'll need a ride," Anna Lee said. "I don't have a car."

"You could ride with me." I offered quickly. I was already basking in the glow of being seen with a local hero, maybe our best and most well-known activist. I didn't want it to end just yet.

"All right."

"We'll meet you down at the Sonorita," I told our friends, referring to a small veggie Mexican restaurant at Speedway and Wilmot. I opened the rider's side for Anna Lee and we climbed in and headed west on Broadway.

The details of our post-demonstration meal mostly escape me now, but I remember Anna Lee's down-to-earth personal and political perspective. I knew that a lot of us, including myself, sometimes loudly postured our radicalism, but Anna Lee was a true activist, living a radical life. She had a quiet confidence and expressed her ideas firmly, but with the volume turned down a good two notches compared to the rest of us. She lived her politics. She didn't have to shout them from the rooftops.

Watching her talk about living in the mountainous countryside above Matagalpa where she worked on a coffee cooperative—one I had actually visited, though not when she was there—made me remember again seeing her for the first time. It was at a pre-demonstration meeting in a local church with some speakers just back from Central America.

She was there with a girlfriend, a really pretty girl, and both of them were probably not that far out of their teens at the time. I remember, despite the other girl's good looks, being attracted to and impressed by Anna Lee. She was a good sized girl, with a noticeable physical presence, but I was just as interested in her behavior.

While the speakers droned on, Anna Lee and her friend—both of whom seemed completely relaxed and somewhat detached from the proceedings—would whisper to each other, shake their heads, and roll their eyes at particularly boring, pretentious, or stodgy moments in the presentation. They didn't disrupt the proceedings in any way but I found their irreverence amusing and refreshing.

Lefty and religious gatherings always seemed to be too dense, heavy, and totally lacking in humor. To see a bright young woman poking holes in the process where it needed them was just fine with me. Somewhere in the middle of some lame discussion of "violence on the right and violence on the left," I saw Anna Lee shake her head in disgust and roll her eyes dramatically at her friend. Shaking their heads, the two young women simply walked out of the meeting. I could barely keep myself from laughing out loud.

• • •

Not long after the Calero demonstration, a group came through town with a film presentation about the death of Ben Linder. Linder had gone to Nicaragua to work much as Anna Lee had. They had actually known each other, I found out, meeting at occasional gatherings of *internacionalistas* in lovely, hilly Matagalpa in the north of the country. Anna Lee worked at the coffee-cooperative. Linder worked in the countryside near the combat zone—an area so dangerous, armed Sandinista troops protected the workers from Washington-supported counter revolutionists called contras.

In spring 1987, Linder's group was ambushed by M-16 carrying contras. In an exchange of gunfire, the young U.S. worker and several of his protectors were killed or wounded. When word of the American's death leaked out, the Reagan administration—working from what evidence no one ever knew—declared Linder a combatant for the Sandinistas, and therefore deserving of his fate.

The group bringing Linder's story around the U.S. had, of course, a very different story to tell.

The small auditorium on the University of Arizona campus where the film and discussion were presented was nearly full—at least one hundred or so people. I arrived with the main crowd. By chance, Anna Lee came up the aisle I was going down and we stopped to visit. She told me about meeting Linder, and I told her about visiting his grave on my last trip to Nicaragua just a few months before. When the presentation began, we found seats together in a row near the front.

The evening went as might have been expected. Plenty of righteous indignation, a number of predictable platitudes, some genuine sorrow. Towards the end, I happened to glance at Anna Lee. I'd tried not to look at her too often, concentrating on the film and speakers so that maybe I would appear appropriately serious—someone who deserved to sit beside someone as decent as she.

What I saw was Anna Lee—possibly the only person in the room who understood Linder, where he'd been, and what he'd done—silently crying. Tears ran down her ruddy cheeks, and her tall body shook ever so slightly. It was a profoundly moving sight.

After several moments more, I forced myself to look away, to let this amazing woman grieve without intrusion. I turned back to the presentation, but I could only think of her and of Ben Linder himself, the once living, breathing human being. I thought of Anna Lee's loss, her grief, of Ben's life, his death, of his other friends' grief and that of his family.

After the presentation, I spoke briefly with Anna Lee and a few friends, but I could not shake the feeling that I was an interloper in some drama I had no right to be part of. Shortly I excused myself and went home alone.

• • •

Some three or four months after the Linder memorial, I reached my saturation point with the spirit-numbing world of computers. I gave a month's notice, worked up until a Thursday night, left Tucson Friday morning, and later that night was sitting on the patio of the Papagayo Hotel in Cuernavaca, state of Morelos, Mexico, sipping on a cold Corona.

I stayed down south for about five months. In a letter from a friend, I heard that Anna Lee had gone back to Nicaragua to continue her volunteer work. When I came back to the States, I learned she'd married a local Nicaraguan guy, a co-op worker like herself.

A couple of years later, while I was living in Colorado, my same friend sent me a newspaper story from a Tucson paper, a nice piece with an interview and photos of Anna Lee showing her life in Nicaragua. About that same time there was a celebrated novel by a well-known Tucson novelist that used the outline and some details of Anna Lee's life for one of its protagonists. Her name, interestingly enough, was left out of the front matter credits where other local progressives of note found theirs.

When I left Colorado a year or two later to come back once again to Tucson, I ran into my old letter writing friend, a long-time local progressive and activist. He told me Anna Lee was still living in Nicaragua and still married. I was glad to hear about her and hoped she was doing well. But I only had the Ben Linder experience to really remember her by, because after that I never saw her again.

Stormy Weather

Gareth "G-Man" Kendall hit Tucson like one of the Sonoran Desert monsoon season thunderstorms he so frequently misforecast. G-Man was all the rage at first. The Old Pueblo was still a pretty small town and he was an exciting new commodity. Although most viewers had no idea his arrival had more to do with his precipitous drop from a mid-major market in Colorado than it did with his perceived meteoric rise in the southern Arizona heavens of broadcast news.

Oh, he was energetic alright. He delivered his five minutes of weather with a big smile beneath his walrus mustache. His portly body shook when he got off a good, safe joke with one of the evening news co-anchors, particularly pretty Sherry Manville. G-Man especially lit up when he and Sherry had their nightly chat that passed for witty journalistic repartee.

The chit-chat, of course, took the attention off the fact that G-Man had no clue whatsoever as to the actual meteorological conditions in southeast Arizona—nor probably anywhere else for that matter.

In point of fact, a trained primate could deliver Tucson's weather forecast most of the year, especially during monsoon season. For the better part of the summer, it was safe to predict that each day would be clear, sunny, and hot with a gradual buildup of cumulous clouds over the cholla and saguaro-filled desert valley floors. Spotty thunderstorms throughout the afternoon, then clear, sunny, and very hot again until sunset. End of forecast. Plug it in, let it sit there, repeat it tomorrow and the day after and the day after...

To his credit, however, G-Man—like all good weathermen—was a character, bad forecasts be damned. He wasn't a magic marker tosser like one of the other "characters" a rival station brought in to do the weather. Rather, G-Man was a character in the sense that he was supposed to be odd, yet safely and humorously so.

Yep, those local weathermen were real cards. G-Man was personable and friendly for sure and he appeared, like the local celebrity that he was, at charity events all around town. Take Back the Night walks, Car Washes for Cancer Research—anything viewed locally as a good cause. Anything that wouldn't get viewers too riled up or anything bad like that.

Ah, but there was a rub. A big one.

The G-Man, it turned out, had a deep dark secret that slowly inched its way out of the shadows of his private life into the garish light of public view. Actually, it was two secrets. One, G-Man had an inordinate affection for that highly popular and highly illegal white substance so many folks in the 1970s and 1980s liked to "candy" up their noses. Cocaine, aka blow, snow, snort, coke, dust, flake—a toot by any name. And second, G-Man developed a human "Jones" as well—for Little Miss Sherry Manville, his comely colleague and evening co-anchor.

At first, G-Man's twin addictions were only the stuff of rumor, innuendo, giggles around the water cooler at the TV station. But, because of his local celebrity status and frequent interactions out and about in the Old Pueblo, the two-pronged problem soon reached out to the consciousness of the city's populace, much like one of his poorly forecast nightly weather reports.

As a generous coke head, G-Man liked to share his extracurricular activity with friends. To his great surprise and joy, it turned out that Sherry Manville liked the white stuff too. How great was that? Soon, G-Man was not only sharing his snow with pretty Sherry but had become her primary connection as well.

G-Man loved to get stoned and he really loved to get stoned with Sherry. She seemed to get progressively friendlier the more dust she blew up her dainty nose—which he gladly provided.

"I just got some really good stuff in," G-Man whispered to her during a commercial break while they were doing the six-o'clock news one fine Friday evening.

He checked to make sure Biff Morgan, the muscled-up sports anchor, wasn't listening. Biff had a case on Sherry, too, and G-Man didn't want some Neanderthal ex-jock horning in on his territory. Sports might be one thing in wooing a lady, but cocaine was a different "trip" altogether. G-Man knew he had the advantage and he wasn't about to lose it. Not to the Biffster anyway.

"This is prime white. Will really get you off," G-Man leered at Sherry. His concupiscence was so overt he was virtually drooling, slobbering as it were, as he took in the curves of Miss Manville's world-class body—the best that money could buy. "If you know what I mean."

Miss Manville giggled. She did know what he meant. Lately he'd been making that clearer and clearer, expecting more and more favors from Sherry and less and less cash for the coke.

"What's all the whisperin' about over there?" The Biffer grumbled. He didn't like that little weather weasel getting so close to Miss Sweet Meat. That was a real man's job. A real man like him—Biff Morgan, the Biffster, the Biffaroni, the Bifforama.

"Professional commentary," G-Man answered with an innocent air. "The lead-in out of the break."

"I bet," Biff countered. "I just bet."

G-Man smiled blankly at Biff, then turned to Sherry with a toothy grin. He pointed out at the main camera as the ten-second countdown began to resume the news. Sherry smoothed her skirt and brushed a hand across the front of her blouse. She had to concentrate on reading the news as she heard G-Man moan just as they went live on-air again.

Over the next weeks and months, G-Man and Sherry got closer and closer. The more coked up she got, the more liberties she allowed her fervent supplier. Soon they were messing around—at least G-Man was—and then almost imperceptibly it seemed to Sherry, she was giving him full access to all she held near and dear. That is to say she started letting him explore that sparkling body of hers.

Finally, in a virtual drug stupor, she let him boff her. Gave the walrus-mustachioed little chunkster her treasured, moist jewel. That turned out not to be such a great idea because not only was G-Man's Jones coke insatiable, but his desire to possess Sherry's downy mound was even more so.

Because she wasn't high all the time, Sherry soon realized it was a bad idea to give the G-Boy so many liberties. And he wasn't really all that good looking, especially when you were coming down from a high and he was lying beside you in a pool of his own sweat, drooling onto his paunchy midsection.

She began trying to avoid the big "G," going so far as to date the equally repulsive Biffster and spending nights with a girlfriend across town when she knew G-Man would most likely drop by her place.

That was all well and good, but Biff didn't do coke, didn't have any coke, didn't even know what coke was—other than a really sweet, caffeine-laden soft drink, which did nothing for a girl used to the pleasure some good white powder could provide.

As the need for stimulation increased, Sherry's attempt to remain independent correspondingly weakened. She let "G" back in her life. She had to. He seemed to have all the coke in Tucson. She attempted to draw the line with him, though. No more sex, unless she really needed to get high.

"No." She admonished G-Man when he made his inevitable advances. "No."

"Please, baby," he begged, his big mustache tinged with white flakes. "I'll give you more. I'll give you all I got."

"No more," Sherry half-heartedly argued.

But there was always more. G-Man made sure of that. He spent every dime he could get his hands on—and more—to keep them in the white stuff. Finally, one weekend afternoon things went south for the couple. Sherry OD'ed with G-Man in the saddle, so to speak.

He didn't realize she lost consciousness at first, so intent was he on his own pleasure. But when he realized she was not only unresponsive but totally limp as well, he started to panic.

"Sherry," he cried, tears running down his round cheeks to mingle among the well-trimmed hairs of his mustache. "Wake up, wake up. Oh, God."

Climbing off his supine partner, G-Man caught a leg in the bedspread and tumbled out onto the thick carpet of Sherry's bedroom floor. He didn't know what to do.

"I don't know what to do," he squawked fearfully, addressing Sherry as if she might lend a hand in his moment of need. "What do I do? What? What?"

"Biffer," Sherry gargled.

"Help, help," G-Man muttered.

He gathered his clothes from a chair near Sherry's bed and hurriedly dressed. Then, Gareth Kendall, the locally famous G-Man, did the only thing his life had prepared him to do. He hauled his rotund ass out of there as fast as he could.

Racing away in his sporty Mazda RX-7, it occurred to G-Man that he should at least try to get someone to take care of Sherry. It was crazy of her to mess up his day like this but he wasn't a vindictive man, he'd call for help. They could take care of her. He had to get away from it all. He knew that for sure.

Twenty minutes after someone called 911 using a breathless, fake high-pitched voice to report a drug overdose, an emergency team was working quickly and efficiently on the semi-conscious Sherry Manville. Thanks to the intervention of an anonymous, long-time Tucson television producer, the overdose story was kept out of the papers and, of course, off the evening news.

Luckily, Sherry recovered fully. She spent a productive month or so in an outpatient drug treatment center on Tucson's northwest side. The staff helped her gain control of her life again. It didn't take many days of therapy for Sherry's head to clear and for her to realize that she actually detested G-Man. She never mentioned him by name but the counselors and fellow patients agreed, whoever did this to pretty Sherry Manville was someone to assiduously avoid.

In a word, Sherry now loathed G-Man, which conversely made him want her all the more. Back on the news set, things became very tense between them. G-Man, sincerely remorseful, tried to win Sherry back. He sent her cards, flowers, candy, and in a lapse of judgement, taste and appropriateness, a male stripper. Sherry rejected them all.

Finally, G-Man could take no more. His unrequited love and spiraling drug habit combined to make him lose it. After a late Friday night newscast and coked completely to the gills, he showed up on Sherry's condo front lawn at 1:15 a. m flailing around a large hunting knife.

"Sherry!" he wailed into the early morning air. "Sherry! Come out. Talk to me. Talk to me."

"I'll talk to you, you crazy son of a bitch," one of Sherry's neighbors yelled at G-Man from the safety of a balcony above the blade-wielding weatherman.

"Stay out of this, Buster," G-Man growled. The neighbor slipped back into his condo with a middle-finger gesture at the lunatic on the lawn.

"Sherry!" G-Man whined and moaned at the closed window of his former squeeze. "Get out here, right now. I'm Gareth Kendall and you're not dumpin' me, you bitch. You need me. You can't live without me. Sherry!"

Sherry was apparently convinced she could live without G-Man, for she called the police. Officers soon arrived. They found the redoubtable weatherman on his knees in the grass of Sherry's neatly mowed lawn meekly waving the knife around.

"Drop the knife, sir," a very patient young officer demanded.

G-Man responded by passing out, the knife falling harmlessly onto the lawn beside him.

"You know who this is?" the young cop's older partner asked.

"No."

"It's Gareth Kendall, the weatherman. You know, G-Man."

"Never heard of him."

"You gotta watch more TV. This guy's a local celebrity."

"Couldn't prove it by me."

"Let's get him in the car and get him downtown," the older officer said. "I don't think the TV station is going to want this to go out on the evening news."

After the arrest on Sherry's lawn that fateful evening, or early morning, Gareth Kendall disappeared from the local TV scene. For local news watchers, he might as well have dropped off the face of the earth. He was just up and gone. For a few weeks after the "lawn incident," rumors flew about what happened to the star-crossed celebrity twosome.

Some said the libidinous G-Man had been sent to the big house—the state penitentiary—in Florence. Others heard that in his unfulfilled state of lust and affection, he himself had OD'ed and was in a treatment center up near Oracle. It was even suggested that G-Man had crossed over to the dark side of the law and was now working for Mexican drug lords south of Hermosillo.

A year or so after the exciting knife-wielding and shouting incident, it was reported by a traveling Tucsonan that while in the Denver area, he saw G-Man doing the weather at a station in the Mile High City. The old weather dog had found his way back home—apparently broadcast stations didn't bother to do background checks on job-jumping journalists these day— and G-Man was back in the biz, so to speak.

The traveler also reported that G-Man acted quite a bit differently than he had in his Tucson days. He was much calmer, lower-key. Probably just happy to have a job and not be in the pen. That was the last report anyone received on Gareth Kendall down in Arizona. He was gone—and shortly forgotten.

As for Sherry Manville, she actually reappeared briefly on the evening news. But the cloud of bad memories and unavoidable publicity left by her connection to G-Man finally enveloped her, too, and one fine day she disappeared from the local airwaves as well. There was never any word about her again. No follow up. It was like she dropped off the face of the planet.

Of course, she was quickly replaced by a prim, young up-and-comer, who was actually introduced by the new, less flamboyant weatherman who, like his unfortunate predecessor, couldn't help but flirt and leer at the nubile, new news gal.

Nowadays the Sherry-G-Man incident, a great moment in Tucson broadcast history, has been lost in the mists of time. Only a few old-timers in town recall the days of Sherry

Manville and Gareth "G-Man" Kendall. More's the pity, as the saying goes, for they were a great pair of TV journalists—their lives providing far better news stories than anything they ever reported on. Oh, yes, far better, indeed.

Train Boarding

Mark Lewis managed to snag the last *camarín* on the overnight train from Mexico City to Guadalajara. The single sleeper-compartment room was small but comfortable and, above all, private.

Around eleven-thirty, Mark lowered the bed in the compartment and settled in for the night. While the train rattled across central Mexico, he drifted off to sleep—images of his recent journeys playing in his mind like a pleasant, colorful movie.

He saw himself standing on the hilltop ruins of Xochicalco, overlooking the distant, desert landscape and much closer below, in the foreground, the ancient ballfield where men once played a game perhaps for life and death. He felt the dry heat against his face, heat that reminded him of Arizona, his native home.

Then he was inside the Palace of Fine Arts in Mexico City viewing the Diego Rivera mural which so easily morphed into the Rivera murals in the national palace in the zocalo, the huge city's central plaza. In particular, he could see the greenish, sickly face of Hernan Cortes, Rivera's most especially hated *conquistador* and artistic subject.

Drifting away from the Palacio Nacional, he saw himself descend a stairway into the metro subway system where he passed fully armed, colorfully dressed Aztec warriors who emerged from beside white rock steps layered in seeping veins of blood. Recoiling from the steps, he heard the click-clacking of the subway train as it approached his stop.

Opening his eyes with a jerking movement, Mark awakened to the real world of the train compartment and to the rattling sound of steel wheel on steel rail. Outside his window, the countryside gave way to houses and little towns as the train neared Guadalajara.

"Whew," he whistled, lifting his head to get a better look out the window. "That was a doozy of a dream. Must've eaten too much before I went to sleep."

By the time the train pulled into the Guadalajara station, Mark had forgotten all about the dreams. He focused on catching the next train to Tepic, where a friend had recommended he catch a bus to the quaint seaside pueblo of San Blas. On the train out of Guadalajara, he sat beside a young Mexican woman a few rows ahead of a talkative American couple.

"*Con permiso?*" he asked the woman before taking the seat.

"*Como no,*" she replied with a friendly smile.

"*Me llamo,* Mark," he said, as the train picked up speed out of Guadalajara. "My name is Mark."

"Daniela." The woman offered him a soft, smooth hand which he gently shook.

"Nice to meet you." He let her slowly remove her hand from his. "You speak Spanish very well."

"*Oh, pues,* no, not really. Like a student or tourist, no better."

Daniela turned away and concentrated on a book she was reading. Mark peeked at its title, but didn't recognize it as anything he might know in English or had studied in Spanish classes back in Cuernavaca. While she read, he occasionally checked her out in profile. She had large brown eyes, shiny black hair weaved in a long pony tail, perfectly tan-colored skin. Classic.

For a good spell, Mark relaxed in his seat, occasionally glancing past Daniela at the countryside outside the train window. The green hillsides passing by reminded him of the lower Midwest but not as tree-filled—a mix of moderate and arid climates in a rolling, climbing terrain.

About an hour into the trip, the train slowed, then ground to a stop at a tiny village. Vendors clambered on board with sandwiches, snacks, and soft drinks. One of them, a tall, bone-thin youngster, stopped next to Mark.

"*Tortas, señor.* Sandwiches? Potato chips? *Fruta?*"

"*Sí,*" Mark said, "I'll take a cheese sandwich."

"*Y para su esposa?*"

"*Mi esposa?* My wife?"

"*Una torta de queso, tambien.*" Daniela said. She did not correct the vendor's use of the term wife.

"And something to drink, missus? Sir?"

"A Sprite," Mark said.

"Orange juice?" Daniela asked.

"*Sí, señora,*" the vendor said, getting the drinks. Daniela smiled at Mark, who still stared at her.

"It was easier to just let him think that," she said with a twinkle in her pretty brown eyes.

"Yeah." Mark opened his bottle of Sprite. "Yeah."

After the meal, Mark made a point of speaking to Daniela. That part about not denying she was his wife thing was intriguing. It was an interesting development, no doubt.

"Where are you from?" He took the refuse from their lunch and put it into a plastic bag at his feet. She nodded her approval of his tidiness. Mark smiled.

"I am from the little town of Rosario. I have been staying with a sick aunt in Guadalajara."

"Is she alright?"

"Yes, thank you. She is now well and I am going home."

"Do you have family there? Mother and father? I don't know Rosario."

"It is south of Mazatlan. Just a little place. My mother and some aunties and uncles live there still. Two brothers and a sister also."

"A big family."

"Yes."

"And your father?"

"He is passed away."

"Oh, I'm sorry."

"Thank you. It has been many years."

"What do you do in Rosario?"

"I work in a small grocery. My uncle's."

"Ah. The family business."

"Sí."

With every passing moment, Mark felt more comfortable with Daniela. It was as if he had known her a long time already. She was pleasant to speak to, to sit beside. She transmitted a sense of informality and intimacy highly unusual for Mexico, especially between a newly introduced man and woman—even more so when the man was a foreigner, a gringo no less. It was remarkable. It was like they actually were a couple, so wife-like or partner-like was the interaction.

"How about you," Daniela asked after a long break in their talk, "I imagine you are a North American—from the United States?"

"Sí," Mark answered. He immediately wondered if he should have claimed he was a Canadian like a friend of his always did when asked by a local. "I'm from the state of Arizona. Near the Mexican border."

"Are you going home now or will you be staying more time here in Mexico?"

Mark concentrated on Daniela's expression, tried to read if there was an oblique opportunity there? Her eyes betrayed nothing. He heard no hint of irony or humor in the tone of her voice. Maybe he was hoping for something—a once in a lifetime lightning in a bottle?

"I'm going to Tepic. I want to go to San Blas before I go home."

"Ah, yes, of course, the jungle boat rides in San Blas. They are well known."

"Yeah, I really like the idea of zooming through the jungle and seeing all the animals and stuff."

"It will be nice."

"You've done it before?"

"Sí."

"Is it something you might want to do again?"

"Perhaps. But not now. I have to get home and back to work."

"Sure."

Mark fantasized a story where Daniela would get off with him in Tepic and they would go on to San Blas together. That was a nice idea—and foolish.

Another, even more foolish idea crept into Mark's mind as the train neared Tepic. What if he went on with her to Rosario? He could rent a cheap hotel room, visit her at her family grocery store, introduce himself to her family, meet her for an intimate evening walk in the town's little plaza. He was sure there would be one. All towns in Mexico, big or small, had a plaza. He would convince her of his good intentions, he would…

The air-splitting cry of the train's whistle broke into Mark's involved reverie. They were coming into Tepic. He heard a loud North American couple gather their gear as the train slowed down coming into the station. Mark looked at Daniela. She smiled at him.

"Your stop," she said sweetly.

"Yes. My stop."

With a lurch, the train halted. Mark sighed and picked up his backpack.

"Goodbye." He extended his hand to Daniela.

"Goodbye, *mi amigo.*" She placed her soft, smooth hand in his. He was wont to release it.

The chattering North American couple clopped by and Mark finally let go of Daniela's hand. She smiled again and then looked away out the window. Mark rose reluctantly and walked off the train. The loud American couple stood on the platform just outside.

"Are you going on to San Blas?" the girl of the pair asked Mark.

"Pardon me?"

"We're going to get a taxi to the bus station if you're going that way," the girl said. "We can split it with you, if you want."

"Yeah," Mark said. "Sure. Split it."

He climbed into a waiting taxi with his new acquaintances, Jon and Sheila Decker of Sedona, Arizona—practically neighbors and oh-so-glad to meet a fellow American traveling so far down into Mexico and one who looked like he knew his way around and...

Out the window, Mark saw a hand-painted sign on a wall: "*Yanqui* Go Home."

That made him laugh. It sounded like something you would see in Central America not in a little out of the way town in some out of the way part of Mexico. He took a quick look back at the train. Of course, he could not see inside where Daniela must be sitting, waiting for the train to take her home to Rosario.

After a couple of excruciating hours with Jon and Sheila at the Tepic station, they boarded the bus for San Blas, a little beach resort. Jon and Sheila found seats up front near the driver. Mark went to the back where he sat among a rancher family heading home to the coast.

The men of the family, all with straw hats, blue jeans, snap-button shirts, and well-worn cowboy boots, nodded their respect when Mark made room for an elderly woman in their group. He helped her settle two large cloth bags in the aisle beside them.

"*Gracias.*" The old woman showed a kind—if scraggle-toothed—smile.

"*De nada,*" Mark replied, triggering the nod from the woman's cowboy relatives.

After the short ride to San Blas, through jungly green hills and over winding roads, the passengers were discharged at the upper part of San Blas near the village church. Mark escaped the Deckers, who bickered for a ride to their hotel, and hoofed it into town to find a hotel of his own.

He was almost immediately accosted by several men offering their services as guides for the jungle boat ride—San Blas' claim to fame. He took the third man's offer and promised to meet him back near the city center at seven-thirty the next morning.

After a quiet night in an inexpensive hotel just off the main street, Mark ate a light breakfast at a small café near the main plaza. No sooner had he paid and started for the meeting point with his guide than he ran into the Deckers. They were with Mark's guide. They were going on the jungle boat ride, too.

"How great we ran into you again," Sheila said with a big, friendly smile.

"Yeah. Great."

The boat ride, despite more commentary from the Deckers than Mark cared for, was actually very good. Right away they all ducked down as the boat passed under a concrete drain serving as a low-lying bridge.

From then on, the journey up an extremely narrow estuary overhung with heavy foliage was remarkable. Tropical birds filled the trees in the mangrove-like backwater. Turtles sunned themselves on partially submerged limbs, snakes moved through the water or clung to small branches, and the occasional crocodile made an appearance. The turnaround-point was a banana plantation with huge clusters of fruit hanging from thick-bodied, tree-sized plants. A nearby open-air restaurant was unexpectedly closed, but overall the trip was quite pleasant. After it was over, Mark even deigned to have supper with the Deckers at McDonald's restaurant in San Blas.

"Not the McDonald's," Jon Decker repeated several times during the meal. "No Golden Arches."

"No Happy Meals," Sheila happily joined in.

"Not a Big Mac in sight," Jon chortled.

"Yeah." Mark sighed. "Same name, not the same restaurant."

"How do they get away with it?" Sheila wondered.

"I wonder?" Jon said, scratching his chin.

"Different country," Mark said, impatiently. "No attempt to duplicate the franchise. Just a name. No McDonald's Police down here to enforce corporate identity laws." The Deckers snickered nervously and looked at each other in commiseration. After dinner Mark escaped as politely as he could.

The next day he lolled about. Rising late, he walked on the beach then took an excursion to the ruins of an old Spanish fort outside town. After another day of doing nothing, he grew restless and decided to move on.

Walking to the bus station on a fine, warm morning, he passed a cathedral and happened to see the same cowboy family he had ridden down with on the bus from Tepic. They again acknowledged him, and he them with a brief nod of recognition and respect. It filled Mark with a sense of belonging, of human interconnection, even though they had scarcely spoken a word to one another. It was the kind of little moment he always remembered from his trips. Just a small flash of fraternity in a world too often lacking it.

A couple of hours later, back at the Tepic train station, Mark bought a one-way ticket to Mazatlan. He stood on the platform in the warm moist air until the signal was given to pull out, then he climbed on board. Walking into the front of his car, Mark was surprised to see the Deckers seated well towards the back.

Oh, my God, he thought, *not again.* He returned the enthusiastic couple's wave with a minimal, tepid one of his own, settling into his seat. No one was sitting beside him, so Mark tossed his backpack onto the empty seat and stretched his legs in front.

Just out of Tepic, the train traversed through hilly, green terrain over tall trestles on its way out of the high country towards the flat land of the coastal plain. The car rocked gently from side to side, and the click-clack noise of iron wheels on steel tracks soon put Mark into a peaceful reverie in which his mind quickly and predictably found its way to an image of pretty Daniela.

He imagined himself in the little town of Rosario, walking along with her on the Sunday evening lover's promenade around the central plaza—a tradition he'd seen followed by the young people in the hill town of San Miguel de Allende, northwest of Mexico City. With this pleasant image in mind, he dozed off until the train began to grind to an unexpected stop.

Focusing his sleep-blurred eyes on the outside world, Mark saw that they were coming into a small station. He caught the name on a sign as the train pulled up to the platform. Ciudad Hidalgo. Expecting an onslaught of vendors hawking food and drink, he sat up to attention when a team of four Mexican soldiers clattered into the car instead. They were in full uniform and carried military rifles.

Anticipating an identity check, Mark reached inside his shirt to the pocket T-shirt underneath where he carried his passport. He held it up for the soldiers to see, but they brushed right by him without so much as a glance his way. Surprised, he turned to watch what they were up to. About midway back in the car, they stopped in front of two small, elderly campesinos—farmers in old clothes and straw hats carrying cloth bags over their shoulders.

The soldiers said something to the little men—very roughly, Mark thought—and signaled for the campesinos to stand. The two men complied, but seemed as confused as everyone else in the car.

The men were turn around and frisked head to toe, all the while being berated in Spanish. One of the farmers raised his hand and spoke briefly, causing a heavy-set soldier to point his rifle at him. Mark heard the rest of the car hold its collective breath.

Then, just when it seemed something terrible might happen, the little farmers lowered their heads in acquiescence. With the tension diffused, the army squad encircled the men and marched them out of the car.

As they passed in front, one of the campesinos glanced at Mark, but the man's eyes betrayed neither fear nor understanding. Mark again held out his passport but the soldiers had no interest whatsoever in him. They marched the campesinos off the train and out of sight into the station. No sooner were they all gone than the Deckers popped up at Mark's side.

"Unbelievable, huh?" Jon asked.

"What the hell was that?" was all Mark could think to say. "What did those little old men do?"

"No telling," Sheila commented. "This is Mexico."

Mark gave her a hard look.

"Maybe they were drug mules," Jon suggested. "Or illegal workers from Guatemala or something.."

"They didn't even look at anybody else. Especially us foreigners," Mark said. "That seemed funny."

"Not good for tourism?" Jon said.

"Maybe it was simpler than that," Sheila remarked. "Maybe they were wanted men. You know, criminals."

"I didn't know the army here did that kind of thing," Mark said. "That's disturbing."

"Well," Jon said, shaking his head, "it's probably better not to think about it."

"What the hell is that supposed to mean?" Mark asked.

"There's no reason to be mean to us about it, you know," Sheila sniffed. "We didn't do it."

"I'm sorry," Mark apologized. "I guess I just haven't seen anything like that before down here."

"The train is getting ready to go again," Jon announced. He and Sheila abruptly left to reclaim their seats.

On the way to the next stop, Daniela's hometown of Rosario, Mark couldn't get the train boarding out of his head.

Why did they go after those little old men? And not one glance at any of the gringos. It was an enigma that could not be answered as simply for him as it seemed to have been for the Deckers. They accepted it as natural and normal. But Mark couldn't get his head around the incident. It was fairly dispiriting.

When the train stopped at Rosario, he hustled out onto the platform ahead of the ubiquitous vendors and away from any possible conversation with the Deckers. From one end of the station he could see a little way into the tiny pueblo, and his pulse jumped when he spotted the word *Abarrotes* painted in white on the clear window of a little store across the road.

"Groceries," he said out loud. "Jeez."

He wondered if the little place might be Daniela's family store. He briefly entertained the idea of going out into Rosario to find out. Even if it wasn't her store, he could go among the people and ask if they knew her, knew where she lived. He would surprise her. Stay longer in Mexico. Stay...

"Whoa, boy," he laughed out loud, shaking his head. "Get it together."

Smiling to himself, Mark climbed back on board the train for Mazatlan and tried to let the image of and the newly imagined encounter with Daniela fade from his mind. There was no way that could happen. He knew it and he knew better.

In Mazatlan, the Deckers—ever the optimistic travelers— invited Mark to join them for another few days before they might all head back to the States together. Mark declined but made sure they knew he appreciated their generosity of spirit.

"Maybe another time," he said, knowing there would never be another time. These unexpected interludes with people on the road were exactly what they seemed—one-time chance encounters. They never developed further. "But thank you. Thanks for putting up with me."

"Good luck, then," Jon told him.

"Goodbye," Shiela said.

"Goodbye to you both, and all the best."

Without looking back, he turned and walked to the ticket window.

"Nogales," he told the lady behind the metal screen. "One way."

The trip to the border was uneventful and Mark rode in near silence. The train pulled into the Nogales, Sonora station around ten-thirty in the morning. Mark grabbed his bag and took a taxi to the border crossing. In just a few minutes, he was in the Nogales, Arizona bus station buying a one-way ticket to Tucson.

Looking out the window of the bus as the familiar desert landscape of saguaro, prickly pear and cholla cactus passed by, Mark sighed in relief to be back home. He wasn't sure what his future held, but there was one thing for certain. He had seen plenty on the trip and now, after a long stretch south of the border, this Mexico trip was over.

For Bread and Milk

"Charles." Dora Evans called from the kitchen. "We need bread and milk."

"We don't have any left?" Charles turned away from the late evening news.

"Just enough for breakfast, dear." Dora took a piece of chocolate pie from the refrigerator. "Do you want a snack?"

"No, no."

"What's the weatherman say?" She rejoined him in the living room.

"He's not on yet."

Charles sat at one end of a large green couch that rested directly in front of the television set. Dora sat beside the couch in a well-padded wicker chair.

"Should you be having that? Your cholestrol."

"The weather will be on next." She ignored his admonition. "They'll tell us if it will snow or not."

"I think it's supposed to snow tomorrow."

"Uh-huh."

"Wish we still had the car," he said. "I hate being old."

"No you don't," Dora laughed. "It gives you license to complain about everything and no one ever contradicts you."

"You do."

"That's my job."

"I still wish we had the car. We could zoom right through the snow."

"The last car we had couldn't 'zoom' through anything. It was two-wheel drive and slid on anything even remotely wet or slick."

"Hmph. You shouldn't have pie this late."

"Please." She rolled her eyes. "I don't believe it matters at our age whether we sneak an extra piece of pie or not. Besides as skinny as you are, you should eat more, anyway."

"Bah."

They had been married over fifty years. Neither recalled much of life prior to their time together. They met in college and fell in love, passionate love. After fifteen childless years, they hit a sour patch. Charles strayed a few times and Dora considered divorce. But no sooner had the patch developed, than it ended. He'd rediscovered his commitment to her, and they passed over the rough spot. They concentrated on their university careers, his as a professor of math, she as a Victorian specialist in the English Department.

Finally, after thirty years together, they settled into a comfortable life of mostly companionship and mutual support. They attended academic functions together, traveled abroad, enjoyed their lives as a well-respected couple on campus. And they grew into a relaxed old age, a warm, golden time highlighted by pleasant company and easy friendships. When they retired from the university, they became each other's constant companions with the matronly Dora's calm personality the perfect counterpoint to scrawny Charles' occasional grumpy frumpiness.

These days, as the couple approached their eighties, life was quiet, almost still. Parties were mostly a thing of the past, old students seldom came by anymore, and the couple relied more and more on each other's company. They breakfasted together, puttered around the house or out in the garden in good weather, walked up the hill to the little store where they bought their groceries. All in all, they found a level of contentment that worked for both of them.

"The weather's starting." Charles waved his arms as if she couldn't see the set six feet in front of her.

"They never get it right, anyway," Dora said, dismissing the chunky, pseudo-meteorologist who appeared on screen with a smile wide enough to endanger the muscles in his jaws.

"Hush."

"We'll see how the weather is in the morning, anyway." She burped loudly.

"See." He pointed at her. "I told you not to eat that pie."

"You hush. I'd better get some orange juice to wash this down with."

"Be better off with a 7-Up."

"You be quiet."

Dora rubbed her chest when she was out of Charles' sight and burped again. She was glad he couldn't see or hear her.

• • •

When they got up next morning, the sky was gray with clouds heavy with snow. Dora made a traditional breakfast of eggs, bacon, toast, and milk and they read the morning paper as they ate. She hid her continued indigestion behind the entertainment and travel pages.

"We still going to the store?" Charles set the sports section down on the table by his dirty plate.

"We need to." She belched quietly into the paper.

"It'll be cold out there. You just had bronchitis for cryin' out loud."

"Worry wart."

"Doctor says you should take it easy."

"Doctor doesn't live here, does he?"

"Hmph. That makes a lot of sense. I wish we still had the car."

"Walking is good for us at our age." She folded the newspaper and set it on the table. She collected all the dishes and took them out to the kitchen.

"I don't know," He said when she returned to the dining area.

"Oh, come on, it'll be an adventure."

"It may snow."

"It is snowing." Dora looked out the living room window. "Apparently has been for a while, too. But it doesn't look like there's much wind and it's not terribly cold."

"How would you know that?"

"It's never terribly cold when it snows. Not around here."

"Oh. Well, we should at least protect our heads."

"I have my scarf and you have your hat."

"Better than that."

"All right, we'll take the umbrellas."

"Umbrellas?" Charles shook his head. "It's snowing, not raining."

"They'll be perfect." Dora assured her husband.

"Hmph."

But he let her collect the umbrellas from a tall, metal canister in a closet by the front door. They kept their coats and boots in the same closet, and Dora drew those out as well.

"Here." She handed Charles his coat, boots, and an umbrella.

"This isn't my umbrella. Mine's black."

"That is black," she assured him, unsnapping the cover strap on her umbrella. "Mine's dark blue."

"If you say so..." He grabbed her arm. "Don't open that indoors, that's bad luck."

"Oh, for heaven's sake, don't be silly."

"Don't do it. It's a bad idea. A really bad idea."

"Very well." She set the umbrella down while they put on their coats and boots.

"Ready?" He asked, when she'd buttoned his coat around the collar for him.

"Ready."

He exited the house first, with her just behind. She loosened her umbrella as she crossed the threshold and let it pop completely open out on the front porch.

"It's really snowing." Charles stepped onto the porch steps.

The snow fell hard, in big beautiful flakes, and accumulated rapidly. There was about three inches on the ground already and the heavy sky promised much more to come.

"We'd better get going, then." Dora suddenly repressed another heavy belch.

They were quiet as they walked down the street, snow crunching pleasantly beneath their winter boots. They had been together so long that sometimes they had no need of conversation. They communicated closeness and caring without words, by simply being together. For all his grumpiness, Charles had no idea what he would do without Dora. And for her part, Dora could not imagine a world without Charles.

As they climbed the hill to Dawson's Grocery Store, the snow plummeted down. It fell so hard, they slogged instead of walked. He grumbled about not having the car again but his grousings went unanswered as she fought the incline. She struggled to catch her breath, felt a tightening in her chest. She stopped and put the back of her hand to her head.

"Are you okay?" He turned back when he realized his wife was no longer alongside him.

"I'm fine," she wheezed. "Just indigestion."

"Still?" He scowled.

"I'll be okay. I'll be fine."

"It's this damnable snow." He waited for her to reach him. "We shouldn't have come. I—"

"Oh," she groaned.

"What's wrong?" He reached for her.

"I'm light-headed, can't breathe..."

Suddenly, Dora simply sat down in the snow in the middle of the sidewalk.

"Oh," she moaned.

Charles was quickly at her side, helped her sit up next to the curb. He took her umbrella and held his over her head.

"Breathe slowly, sweetheart."

"I feel so weak."

"I'll get help."

"Please don't leave me."

"I won't," he said.

At that moment, a lady from a nearby house, about their, came out to see what was the matter.

"Please, ma'am," He called to her. "Please call for help. Call 911."

The lady hurried back inside. Charles turned to Dora.

"Stay with me, Dora," he said gently. "Please stay."

He knelt beside her, let her rest her body against his. Her breathing was erratic and difficult. He kept his umbrella over them. The snow kept falling, heavily.

In less than ten minutes, the paramedics arrived. A young man and young woman, both of them strong, bright-faced, and very efficient, immediately took charge of the situation. They did their best to stabilize Dora, to control her breathing, to make her comfortable. When they had gotten her into their vehicle they laid her down on an emergency cot, put a warm blanket around her and hooked an oxygen mask to her face.

The young woman helped Charles up into the vehicle for the ride to the hospital.

"What were you folks doing out on a day like today?" the emergency room doctor asked Charles after he hooked up Dora to all the proper monitoring devices and she was resting comfortably. "This was hardly the day for an early morning stroll."

"We were going to the store for bread and milk," Charles explained. "We don't have a car."

"Couldn't someone have gone for you?"

The doctor was fresh out of med school, filled with a righteous desire for people to take care of themselves. It was the cornerstone of a good healthy life, he believed. Seeing these old people out doing something so foolish as walking in a heavy snow, seemed pretty peculiar to him—and counterproductive to their health.

"My wife likes to walk," Charles told the doctor, "and we had our umbrellas."

"Umbrellas in the snow?" The doctor did his best to control an ironic smile. "Well, when it's bad weather like this just be more careful."

"Uh-huh," Charles nodded.

"Your wife will be fine." The doctor put his arm around his shoulder. "We'll need to keep her here for a couple of days to make sure her breathing gets nice and smooth and we'll take some tests of her heart. She should make a full recovery. I'll have our nutritionist recommend a better diet perhaps and a slow lead-in to an exercise program. At least in good weather she may be able to try that hill again. But not for a while."

"No," he agreed. "Not for a while."

"I've had the front desk call a taxi for you, Mr. Evans. The snow isn't letting up any and you'll need a ride home I'm sure."

"Yes, thank you."

"There is a service in town that gives elderly folks rides. I'll have our people call them for you if you'd like. That way you can come in whenever you wish over the next couple of days to see your wife. I would imagine you might want to come back in the morning. We'd like her to rest by herself tonight."

"Yes, yes. That will be fine."

"Very well, then," the doctor said as they reached the front desk, "our people will take care of all that for you, sir."

"Thank you."

A young woman at the desk smiled patronizingly at him and the doctor hurried back to his work. Charles sighed.

•   •   •

Charles stood on the front porch knocking snow off his boots before entering the house. He shook the moisture off the umbrellas, closed, and snapped their straps shut. Then he went inside. In the long hallway leading into the house, he paused and listened. It was so quiet and empty within that he thought for a moment he would cry.

He prayed to whatever power there was that he would precede Dora in death. He could see no way in which he could stand this terrible silence of nothing. He knew that without her, life would have neither purpose nor meaning.

Opening the hall closet, Charles prepared to put away the umbrellas. He knew that carrying those damnable things had been a bad idea—it was just plain bad luck. Unceremoniously, he deposited them in their tall metal storage canister. He was glad to be rid of them. He wouldn't use umbrellas in the snow again. Not as long as he lived.

Fallen

Jim Finerty had been writing so long he couldn't recall when he started. It was sometime when he was a kid, he was pretty sure of that. His mother nurtured his creative side from a very young age. Some of his earliest memories were of her patiently reading books and newspapers to him until, very soon, he began reading for himself. In fact, he could not remember when he actually learned to read. It was a skill that had always been there—thanks to his mother.

But where Jim's mother was positive and optimistic, he went the other way. A plaque on the wall behind his writing desk contained the tenets of his philosophy.

There is no such thing as security

No one gets out alive

There are no happy endings

Friends and family pointed out the seemingly negative nature of such a philosophy, but Jim considered this tripartite view of life to be flatly realistic. It was what it was. Neither positive nor negative.

Jim's writing career, as it were, had progressed in fits and starts. In grade school, like innumerable children before and after him, he created little stories for his mother. His first foray into a larger work, though, came in the sixth grade. Spurred by one of his friends who also harbored dreams of being a writer, Jim wrote a sports novel. Terrible as the work turned out — extravagantly awful—it was nonetheless a complete book. At least for a twelve-year old.

For the next several years, Jim rested on his laurels—so to speak. That is to say, he didn't do much creative writing. Not because he wouldn't have wanted to, but because no writing ideas occurred to him. He wanted to be a writer, but he wasn't exactly sure how to go about it. During his service years, the urge to create was on a back burner to drinking, bars, and women—but he still told his best buddies that he wanted to be a writer.

Finally, out of the military and into college, Jim put pen to paper and began writing in earnest. His early efforts were often false starts, poorly done or incomplete, and universally unsuccessful. But as an adult he discovered that he really had it—the scribbler's disease. He could not but write. He threw away many of his early tries at poetry and fiction, but he always began again. Always. So he wrote. And wrote something else. And wrote again, and again. Always moving on, always hoping to find his own voice, to settle into a style of his own. One that would be his and his alone. The voice of Jim Finerty, writer.

After a few years more, the finished works began to pile up. Novels, books of short stories, a small group of poems, attempts at screenplays. He found the voice he'd searched and hoped for. That discovery, though, gave him no special luck in either selling his work or even seeing it published in non-paying literary journals. Jim, like thousands of other writers, soon had enough ego-deflating rejection slips to paper his walls.

Along the way, to paraphrase the country song, he lost a wife and a girlfriend. The wife simply tired of the game. It seemed romantic and hopeful in the young days, but years and years of unrelenting failure took its toll. She finally chose to go her own way, leaving Jim to his compulsive writing and stacks of rejections. The girlfriend missed the youthful, optimistic days, and the prospect of sharing the mid-life phase of a failed writer's life seemed bleak indeed. Like the wife before, she simply left.

Alone now, Jim concentrated exclusively on his writing and started to have some success. Not a lot, but a little. Slowly it built. A few poems appeared in literary journals, he sold a couple of stories to paying magazines, got an agent and sold a novella that was mostly ignored—but was at least out there. Then, in a stroke, he got what he'd hoped for his entire life. He sold a novel to a big publishing house.

Sales for the book started flat, but slowly grew. Local newspapers began calling for feature stories about the new local writing sensation. Radio stations interviewed him. There were readings at libraries and writing clubs—and the book kept selling. Finally, there came a favorable review in a national journal, and the book found wings. It reached the Top 20. High powered literary agencies called him. Decently-sized checks began to roll in on a semi-regular basis. His publisher called to invite him to New York City, to have a kickoff party for a national book tour.

• • •

"You finally did it, buddy. You wrote the big one." Mike Ennis gave Jim a high five.

Mike had read a story about Jim in the town paper that morning and hustled over to congratulate his long-time friend.

He found him where he often was, in the middle of a new writing project, a short story.

"How does it feel?"

"It feels great." Jim smiled.

"I bet it does. Now you'll have a chance to live out your old dream."

"My what?"

"You know, what you always said you'd do if you ever sold a book."

"Huh?"

"You've been telling me for years." Mike wagged a finger at him. "If you ever sold a book or screenplay or anything big like that, that if you sold it on a Friday, you wanted to be found the next Monday semi-conscious in a pool of alcohol, drugs, and starlets."

Jim laughed. "I forgot about that."

"I can't believe you forgot it. You used to say it all the time."

"I was a lot younger then."

"You said it about two weeks ago."

"Did I?"

"Yep."

"Well, as far as philosophies go, it's not such a bad one."

"This is your chance, then, to put philosophy into action. That is, if you weren't just kidding. You'd never really do something like that would you?"

"I'm too old now. I don't think I could cut the mustard anymore. It does show that I have my values all squared away though, right?"

"Oh, yeah," Mike chuckled. "What a commitment to your art. What integrity. A real tribute to all the starving people out there who've ever starved for their art."

"Very funny, my redundant friend."

"You're a silly dude, even if you are a terrific writer."

"I thank you and agree with you, on both counts."

"Ah, the humble author on the cusp of international fame."

"Or on the cusp of just getting enough royalties to rent a decent house. How about that?"

"You'll let me know how the weekend with the starlets turns out?"

"I'll write a story about it for you. Good enough?"

"Good enough."

"Now, if you will pardon me," Jim told his friend, "while I appreciate your support, I really do have to get back to work."

"Dismissed by the great writer."

"We're going to have dinner together this evening. I wouldn't exactly call that being dismissed."

"Alright, Big Shot. I'll catch you later, but you have to promise to tell me your plan for the booze, drugs, and starlet thing. I may be your biographer, you know. Boswell to Johnson as it were."

"More like Shemp to Curley, if you ask me."

"More like," Mike said, letting himself out. "More like."

• • •

At first, New York was thrilling. Jim was wined and dined and toasted and greeted as a not-quite-so-Young Lion. Stephen Burton, the Vice-President for Literary Acquisitions at the Eighty-Second Street Press (New York, New York), scheduled him for photo shoots, artsy brunches and cocktail parties, radio, TV and print interviews. It was a whirlwind of activity capped off by several readings at museums, libraries, and local literary clubs.

Jim found the world of the New York literati to be exhilarating, sometimes exhausting, but extremely stimulating overall. As he imagined in his fantasies, there were women, booze, and dope everywhere he turned and anywhere he went.

At first he took it easy, kept a proper distance from the entropic world awaiting the unwary newcomer. Within a week, however, Jim tried out anything available to a new author with a growing reputation in the Big, Bad Apple.

After tasting the wares of a few literary groupies, he fell in with a ravishing debutante divorcé, a woman of nice sensibilities but flexible morals. Soon, he acted out his supposed joke catchphrase—each day started with new resolutions to straighten up, to toe the line, but every evening ended with the same dizzying conclusion—the haze of alcohol, smoke, and sex he formerly made a joke of.

He spent money like it was going out of style. Heady stuff. And it felt great. So great that he missed some of the scheduled events Steve Burton lined up for him. There was a book signing at a large, chain book store and then a reading at a Manhattan museum. Jim was a no-show at both. Burton worried, tried to rein him in.

"It's for you." The divorcé yawned. The bed covers dropped off her shoulders as she picked up the ringing room phone.

Jim admired her surgically-perfect breasts as she reached out an arm. He waved the call off, lunging instead in an attempt to capture one of those superbly-sculpted breasts in his hand.

"Stop." She swatted at him with her free hand. "Answer this call."

"Mmmh," he groaned, burying his head on her chest. "Yumm."

The woman tossed the phone at him, leapt out of bed, and ran towards the bathroom. Jim moaned as he watched her also-perfect bottom moving up and down as she jogged away. Her body was without doubt, the best that money could buy.

"Yeah," Jim grunted, when the woman was out of sight and he was forced to deal with the phone call. He hoped it was nothing more than room service or the dry cleaners.

"Jim." It was Steve Burton.

"Uh."

"Listen, Jim, what are you doing?"

"Talking to you."

"Very funny. Be serious."

"About what?"

"You can't go missing when we're trying to sell your book."

"I'm not missing. You found me."

"You know what I mean."

"No, I don't."

"You've missed two straight scheduled events. It makes you look irresponsible. It hurts book sales."

"You're making millions off my book," Jim countered as the divorcé came back out of the bathroom, wearing a robe loosely tied at the waist. Jim motioned for her to come back to the bed. She wagged a finger but slowly padded over towards him.

"Not exactly," Steve corrected his writer. "Not even close."

"You're doing all right."

"We can do a heck of a lot better if the author puts everything he has into the promotion of the book, too."

"Sure," Jim said, grabbing the divorcé by the soft belt of her robe. He drug the woman onto the bed and tore open the robe with his free hand, bending to briefly kiss one of her breasts. "That's what I'm doing right now." The woman giggled as Jim massaged her breasts.

"It certainly sounds like it."

"I'm on it, Steve." Jim reached between the woman's legs. She moaned loudly. "No problem. You don't have to worry."

"I know I don't. I've taken care of it."

"What?" Jim pulled himself away from the divorcé. The woman puckered her lips petulantly. Jim stroked her inner thigh, getting a loud sigh for his efforts. "What do you mean?"

"What I mean is, you're going on a book tour. Away from the temptations of New York. Back onto the right path for your career."

"The right path?"

"The right path."

"Very zen."

"Very."

"When?" Jim stood and walked away from his current New York temptation.

"Day after tomorrow. And I'm going along to keep you company."

"Well, for crying out loud."

• • •

The tour started in Chicago, where the publisher limited his writer's behavior to a mild drunk and a couple of inappropriate pawings of young coeds. The next stop was Miami.

There, after a tipsy, slightly incoherent reading and subsequent chaotic book signing, Jim slipped away to South Beach in a limousine. In the private room of a strip club he sampled the strippers' wares for three hours before Steve tracked him down. The executive threw Jim into a cheap cab, took him back to their more prosaic hotel in Miami Beach, and tucked the writer safely in bed.

New Orleans was the next stop and Steve worried about what Jim might try in the Crescent City. Surprisingly, things actually went quite well—at first. Jim gave a good reading and sold a lot of books. Things were looking up.

Then Steve got the call.

"Family emergency," he explained. "I have to get back to New York right away."

"What is it?" Jim asked.

He seemed sincerely worried. Yet not so much so he hadn't managed to already pick up a pretty New Orleans lady.

She apparently had shown a considerable interest in Jim's perceived written and oral skills.

"My mother is ill. I've got to get the next plane out. I'll have my office postpone the rest of the tour."

"Don't do that," Jim said, the lovely Louisiana woman standing close by his side. Her light brown skin juxtaposed against Jim's washed out white. "I'll be all right. I can finish it up. We only have what, three or four cities left?"

"Three, but I don't think..."

"I swear I'll be good." Jim winked at his companion. "Honest."

"I've got to go. Are you sure you'll be alright."

"Go, it's your mom. Don't even think about me. I can look after my own affairs."

That's what I'm afraid of. Steve thought, but didn't say out loud. That's exactly what I'm afraid of.

Kept active by his New Orleans woman, Jim completely missed the Dallas stop—leaving Steve to do the apologizing cross-country. Then in Tucson, Jim got so drunk he actually passed out at a dinner held in his honor, landing face first in a plate of mashed potatoes and vegetables. The Tucson bookstore people were not amused, and canceled the remainder of the stop altogether. In Los Angeles, however, Jim finally reached the bottom. The police report said it all.

"911 call from residence of Mr. Hugh Hefner. Private security personnel reported the suspect, James A. Finerty, writer, no address given, refused to leave grounds of the residence. Suspect scuffled with security, slightly injuring two men, before he (Mr. Finerty) was physically subdued. Mr. Finerty has been charged with simple assault, public lewdness, public drunkenness, being under the influence of controlled substances —marijuana and cocaine— and trespassing. Charges of sexual assault on three young female residents at the address were not pursued."

Fortunately, Jim Finerty was not famous enough for the report to make it onto television, just into the back pages of a few tabloids starving for material. But that was enough. Enough to cancel the book tour, enough to make Eighty-Second Street Press drop its promotion of Jim's book and terminate his contract.

• • •

Back home, Jim maintained a low profile during the months after his debacle in Los Angeles. He had been face-to-face with real success, had embraced it, been seduced by it, and through his own volition been corrupted, consumed, and defeated by it. Time to take stock of his life again and rededicate himself as a writer.

To remind himself never to repeat his failures, Jim added another small plaque beside the one listing his three-pronged philosophy of life. To one side of his admonitions about the lack of security and happy endings in life and that no one escaped its final destination, Jim placed his favorite passage from Joyce's *A Portrait of the Artist as a Young Man.*

> *The snares of the world were its ways of sin. He would fall. He had not yet fallen but he would fall silently, in an instant. Not to fall was too hard, too hard: and he felt the silent lapse of his soul, as it would be at some instant to come, falling, falling but not yet fallen, still unfallen but about to fall.*

Such a beautiful passage, Jim thought, *so perfect in its message, so perfectly written.* It was perhaps the most beautiful paragraph in all of English literature. He only wished he had heeded it when the last novel broke big. Instead, he pursued his own ridiculous, hedonistic philosophy and destroyed all the literary gains he'd made. If he could just get a second chance.

"Maybe you'll get a second chance," Mike Ennis consoled his humbled friend.

"Isn't it pretty to think so," Jim countered, using a line from yet another of his literary heroes.

"I don't get it." Mike missed the allusion.

"Never mind, just me trying to be all hip and literary."

"You don't have to do stuff like that, man, you're a good writer, a darned good writer. You'll hit again. I know you will."

"Thanks, buddy."

Mike had stuck by Jim through the rise up and the fall down. You couldn't ask more of a friend.

"But this time, you'll do it right. None of that degeneration stuff. I bet you got that out of your system, right?"

"Right," Jim said.

He tried very hard to keep his nose to the grindstone these days, concentrating exclusively on producing the best fiction he could, ignoring the distractions of the process as fully as possible.

"I have faith in you," Mike said.

"You really do, don't you?"

"Absolutely," Mike affirmed. "Absolutely."

• • •

Buoyed by a newfound discipline and the goodwill of friends like Mike, Jim went back to work on his next book. He felt good, dedicated, disciplined. It seemed he had licked the demons that overwhelmed him with his first, recent success. He was confident he was headed in the right direction once more. The new book, if written with honesty, if written right, would get him back on top, put him back on the right path. Stephen Burton's way of zen.

But the book did not come easy. It was a labor of love, but a

Herculean labor nonetheless. Jim fought for every paragraph, for every page. He dug down deep inside for the words, for the ideas. They came slow—but steadily. A month passed, two, more. Finally, after nearly a year of exhausting mental work, it was complete. He had done it. He had written another novel. And it was good.

Just like before, Jim shipped the new book around—to publishing houses, to agents, to anyone willing to take a look at it. Another month passed, and on and on. Rejections piled up. He recalled again the old joke about writers being able to paper their walls with rejection slips. He understood it was not really a joke. Not to a serious writer.

Then, just as he despaired of ever getting in print again, he got another break. He landed an agent. A likeable, efficient, and seemingly honest agent, Marie Carthon, from New York City.

Marie acted as if she believed in Jim's work, that it was good, that it was important, that it actually might make some money. She was also confident she could get him a book contract, and with her Hollywood connections, was equally certain she could sell the rights to a producer she knew. Jim was thrilled but worried Marie or her producer friend might have heard of his fiasco in L.A.

Failing that, the only fly in the ointment Jim could see was that the film world would have even more temptations than the literary one. He wondered if he could stand up to those temptations again. Could he resist sex, drugs, and alcohol on a major scale?

A shiver ran down his spine at the thought of the beautiful women in L.A. They seemed to produce them there én masse. Like a cookie cutter production line. Like an assembly factory. They were oh so tempting. And resistance to temptation was not his long suit.

In fact, Jim wasn't sure he had a long suit of any kind, but he was trying. He was getting better at patience, the lengthy time it took to write the new novel bore that out, but he still had the writer's itch to create a decent book. He wanted to reach an audience, be successful, make a sale. And once again, just as he felt the sting of incipient despair, his agent called.

"Jim." Marie's voice was as upbeat as always. "Are you sitting down?"

"Yes I am." He pushed his lower back against the lumbar support on his inexpensive desk chair and removed his hands from the keyboard of his laptop. He was busy outlining novel number three. Like every other writer, he had to move on to the next project no matter what happened to the previous one. It was what writers did.

"We've sold the screen rights to your book." Marie said.

"You sold the screen rights to the book?"

"Yes, we did."

"Really?"

"Really."

Jim let the information sink in. He felt a sense of euphoria welling up inside.

"For h...how much?"

"Hold your breath."

"I am. I am."

"You'll never believe it."

"Marie, please, tell me."

"Ready?"

"Ready."

"Two hundred thousand."

"What? Oh, my God. I can't believe it."

"I said you wouldn't believe it."

"That's the most amazing thing I've ever heard in my life."

"Congratulations," Marie said. "You deserve this."

"I don't know about that, but I'll sure as heck take it."

"How soon can you come out to Los Angeles? I'll take you around to see the money men. Does that work for you?"

Jim considered the offer. Two hundred thousand dollars. A prime time agent. Hollywood producers. Could he handle it? Could he make it this time without destroying himself?

He thought about his mottos, his quotation from Joyce. "The snares of the world were its ways of sin. He would fall. He had not yet fallen but he would fall silently, in an instant."

He knew the risks he ran. He knew his own character. Thinking of his second chance at success made the hair on the back of his neck stand up. He had goose bumps on his arms.

"Jim?" Marie prompted.

"Yes," he said, shuddering, "that works for me."

"Good, I'll have my people do your arrangements. We'll be there to pick you up."

"I'll be there." Jim reached over to turn the James Joyce quotation plaque around where he could no longer read it. "Nothing will stop me this time."

J.B.
HOGAN

J. B. Hogan is a prolific and award-winning author. He grew up in Fayetteville, Arkansas, but moved to Southern California in 1961 before entering the U. S. Air Force in 1964. After the military, he went back to college, receiving a Ph.D. in English from Arizona State University in 1979.

J. B. has published over 250 stories and poems. His novels, *The Apostate, Living Behind Time* and *Losing Cotton*—as well as his local baseball history book, *Angels in the Ozarks,* and a collection of his poetry and short fiction entitled *The Rubicon*—are available at Amazon, iBooks, and Barnes & Noble.

J. B. currently serves as Past President of the Washington County (AR) Historical Society. He plays upright bass in East of Zion, a family band that specializes in bluegrass-flavored Americana music.

Facebook: J.B. Hogan
www.thejbhogan.com

THE RUBICON

poems and short fiction

J.B. HOGAN

B reed felt McNair grab his arm. "Quiet," he said.
"What?"
"Quiet."

Breed listened. There was nothing for maybe five seconds, then a weird, distant droning sound rose up and died away. It sounded, if anything, like the continual buzzing of a summer locust.

"What the hell was that?"

"Quiet," McNair said again.

Breed gently set down the wedge of rock that was in his hands.

He had a neckerchief wrapped around his mouth because they were kicking up so much dust digging through the rubble. Cloudsof it drifted like fog in the light of the lantern. McNair's face was pale, his eyes huge and wet. His lower lip was trembling.

There was another noise now.

Something was circling around them out there, moving over the rocks with a ticking sound like a cat's claws will make on linoleum when they're not retracted. *Tick, tick, tick, ticka-ticka- tick.* Now the sounds stopped as if what had made them became aware that they were listening for it.

"What's that smell?" Breed said, pulling down his neckerchief.

But McNair shushed him. Whatever it was, it was thick in the air, a smell of age and dryness like the hot, dead stink of attics and sealed trunks. They both stood there, listening. Breed felt the sweat on his brow begin to run down his cheeks. He licked his lips. He did not know exactly where their visitor was, but he could feel its nearness, sense its presence along his spine. He expected that any moment it would leap out at him, snarling and gibbering, a furry and elfin form with gnashing yellow teeth.